UNEXPECTEDLY IN LOVE

A SECOND CHANCE SINGLE MOM CHRISTMAS ROMANCE

JEAN ORAM

Unexpectedly in Love
A Second Chance Single Mom Christmas Romance

Christmas Mountain Clean Romance Series
(Book 6)
By Jean Oram

© 2019 Jean Oram

Printed in the United States of America unless otherwise stated on the last page of this book. Published by Oram Productions Alberta, Canada.

Complete cataloguing information available online or upon request.

Oram, Jean.

Unexpectedly in Love: Christmas Mountain Clean Romance Series / Jean Oram. —1st. ed.

ISBN: 978-1-989359-06-8 (paperback)

Ebook ISBN: 978-1-989359-06-8

Summary: When single mom Joy Evans returns to her hometown of Christmas Mountain she doesn't expect to fall in love with the man next door. Especially since he has always had a way of getting under her skin… Will Christmas wishes come true for these two opposites as they find themselves unexpectedly in love?

First Oram Productions Edition: October 2019

1019

ACKNOWLEDGMENTS

A big thank you to my team of early readers, Margaret C., Donna W, Erica H, and Sharon S. You gals rock my world. As well, thank you to Margaret C. (a different Margaret!) for all your notes and corrections. You help my stories tie up those little threads I think I've tied up but haven't. And thank you to my proofreaders and series continuity editors Emily, Lia, and Sonya for catching the small things that slipped past, and to my HEAs who put on a few more final touches.

As well, thank you to Susan Hatler, Ciara Knight, Melinda Curtis and Shanna Hatfield for inviting me into the delightfully fun world of Christmas Mountain. It's an honor to write with you in the Rockies—one of my favorite areas of the world.

Most of all thank you to each and every one of my readers. This dream would be nothing but dust without you. I hope this story charms you as well as brings you to both laughter and tears.

To happily ever afters and the warmness of the holiday season.

CHAPTER 1

I adored the holiday season. Not just because of my festive name, Joy Noelle Evans, and because my birthday fell on a date halfway to Christmas, but because I believed the holidays brought everyone together, highlighting their innate kindness and generosity.

Today, however, I wasn't feeling my usual level of holiday joy. I also wasn't feeling the tips of my fingers, due to the frigid December air here in the town of Christmas Mountain, Montana. The colored lights I was stringing along the eaves kept tangling, leaving me frustrated.

As I contemplated the lights again, I caught a glimpse of my seven-year-old son as he tore by with his elbow out—a sure sign he was attempting another running wrestling flop onto the inflatable snowman sitting in the front yard.

"Max, cut it out! You're going to wreck poor Frosty."

"He had it coming! He's a wily, frozen-headed monster! He stuck his tongue out at Ms. Smith when she walked by."

"Max, you better not have done that, too!"

There was a telling silence and my shoulders sagged. Judith Smith was a ruthless gossip who had a hobby of pumping people for information so she could spread it about town. She was well-intentioned, but the last thing I needed was for Max and myself to wind up on her radar—for any reason.

"What have I said about being polite?" I called.

"Okay. I will."

"No sticking your tongue out at people, and next time you see her you need to apologize."

"She didn't see me."

"It doesn't matter."

I readjusted the ladder, wondering where Max had learned his wrestling moves. Surely not from his father, Calvin, a mild-mannered man who was on the same parenting page as I was. Other single moms worried about the influence of their children's fathers and their lax rules, but I knew Max had the same boundaries at Calvin's, which meant no wrestling. No sticking out of tongues, either.

Up on the ladder again, I could see that Max had somehow managed to wrangle the seven-foot-tall snowman into a head-lock, and our golden retriever, who Max had named Obi-Wan Kenobi after the *Star Wars* character, was barking and dancing as though a stranger had entered the yard.

"What was I thinking, buying that snowman?" I muttered to myself. "Obi, hush! And Max, cut it out. You're getting the dog all excited!"

Something caught my eye as our retriever continued to bark. There *was* a stranger, although not in our yard. The new neighbor, whom I'd yet to meet, was rolling some fancy grill, which had likely cost as much as all the furniture in my living room, from his truck, then behind the fence and hedge that separated us, and around to the back of his house. He had a lanky build and improbably wide shoulders. He also had a familiarity that made me think of someone... Someone who didn't bring up entirely pleasant memories.

It *couldn't* be Steve Jorgensen. Like Calvin and me, he'd left town after high school. In fact, the last time I'd seen Steve he'd been smirking from his spot across the street from the police station as I'd shuffled out with my parents, completely mortified, my shoulders hunched to my ears as I'd tried to hide. My friends from Ms. King's choir group and I had released a few pigs down the high school hallway after our graduation ceremony and gotten caught. After that night we'd all gone our separate ways, despite our promise to Ms. King that we'd stick together.

But back to the man next door. He couldn't be Steve which meant I needed to shove aside my introverted nature and bring him a plate of gingerbread cookies. Not the burned ones, or the ones where Max had gone nuts with the icing, but the prettier ones that I'd taken some time with.

The man came back through his side yard, causing Obi to bark again. Our new neighbor snugged the zipper of his coat farther up under his chin as he walked. Due to the distance between our houses, I couldn't quite catch his features even from my higher-than-usual vantage point on top of the ladder.

The man turned as Obi let out another bark, and I caught his familiar blue-eyed gaze. I let out a yelp as my foot slipped on the ladder rung, nearly sending me tumbling.

It *was* Steve. Steve Jorgensen.

No, no, no, no. No...! my mind howled. What had I done to deserve him as my neighbor? I was a good person. Karma should be on my side, not against me!

I didn't dare look back his way as I carefully climbed down to the safety of the frozen earth. It was simply my imagination playing games with me, because why would Steve return to this small, quiet town when he was all about noise and adventure?

Back on solid ground, I cringed and dared a glance over my shoulder toward Maybe-Steve's house. I could no longer see him or his walkway, due to the fence and hedge.

Maybe he'd turned away before I'd slipped.

Not that it had been Steve. There were plenty of men who

were handsome like Steve had been—if his cocky, know-it-all opinion about my life hadn't overshadowed the whole typical good-looks thing he'd had going on.

Man, if he could see me now—with my lovely, peaceful life—his sharp, bright eyes would be brimming with judgment. For all his smarts, he hadn't been able to comprehend why I hadn't continued chasing my dream of medical school, and had instead fulfilled my plan to marry Calvin once out of high school.

In fact, marriage and starting a family had been pretty perfect until Calvin and I had discovered that what we had was friendship and not actually true love. Now we were back in Christmas Mountain, in separate homes and co-parenting cohesively, as well as considering a move to Paris, France so Calvin could pursue an engineering project.

Steve could put adventure in his pipe and smoke it. I was not idly accepting some boring, stagnant life just because I had followed Calvin to college. I wasn't complaisant, like Steve had claimed, unable to accept my life as anything more than what was in front of me. Calvin and I had worked hard for what we had, which was surely more than Mr. Judgy-Pants Adventure had in his hollow, empty, meaningless life.

The old anger burned through me, renewed. Steve had even been there the moment my life dreams had changed, but like everyone else, he hadn't seen why I'd had to give up medical school.

It was a good thing it wasn't Steve next door, because the last thing I needed was him prodding me to change my very happy, quiet life.

IT WAS STEVE.

I knew it the second his boot came around the edge of the white fence that separated our properties—even before his upper body was visible. Obi-Wan was barking, but his dancing around faded from my attention due to the concern in those same blue eyes of Steve's that had once held such scorn.

The judgment would be back soon. I was a single mom with student loans and a job that left me constantly strapped for cash.

"Joy? Are you okay?" Steve asked. "Joy?" He was reaching for my arms as if he planned to catch me. "I saw you slip."

I wrenched my hands back to my sides, having extended them toward him.

"Steve?" I cringed inwardly. I was not acting the way I'd dreamed I would if we ever met up again. In those fantasies my life was casually flaunted in his face. He would look at me with awe and a bit of envy for having a family and... and love.

My chest ached.

"Hey, how's it going?" I asked, playing it cool while giving Obi the hand signal for him to sit and be quiet beside me, which he did.

"Are you okay?"

"Yes! Of course." I glanced over at his house and tried to swallow the gut-dropping feeling I was experiencing. "Are you...?" I couldn't find the courage to ask the question barging through my mind.

Besides, I didn't have to ask; I knew the answer. I'd seen the For Sale sign come down, and through the crack in my curtains I'd watched the moving truck roll up.

Steve Jorgensen lived next door, and Paris, despite my lack of second-language skills, was starting to look mighty appealing for more than just staying close to my son. I'd learned every bone in the human body by age thirteen, so I could certainly learn French at age twenty-seven. Happily.

"Am I your neighbor?" Steve finished stating my earlier question, crossing his arms and watching my reaction. His expression was devoid of emotion, the crossed arms a defensive mechanism. One that I was exhibiting, as well.

"Welcome to the neighborhood." I gave what might have passed as a friendly smile among T-rexes, and turned to deal with the dangling Christmas lights so I could have a moment to process his presence in my life. Obi, no longer perturbed by Steve's arrival due to a healthy, vigorous ear rub from said man, went off to find Max.

Seeing Steve again was worse than the moment I'd pulled his name out of Mr. Chen's hat in biology class, locking me in as Steve's secret Santa—hadn't it been bad enough to be partnered with him in chemistry? I'd agonized over what to get him. It would have been easy to pick up a cheap trinket or some candy, but for some reason I'd gone into obsession mode. It had felt as though Steve needed more than a meaningless bit of junk, and in the end I'd purchased him a pocketknife that had cost more than the T-shirt I'd bought for Calvin.

As far as I knew, Steve still didn't know who'd given him the knife. Thankfully. He probably would have found a way to criticize me for the expenditure.

"How long have you been back?" he asked as I climbed the ladder. He fed me the string of lights while I attached them to the eaves.

Why couldn't he just walk off and stay away instead of being helpful? Was he in need of fresh fodder so he could renew his hobby of judging me?

"A year," I muttered grudgingly, when he continued to help.

"How's Christmas Mountain? Has it changed much?"

It had. It had been on the last downhill run toward ghost town status when I'd been summoned back to play the piano for The Christmas Extravaganza with the girls last year. It had been Ms. King's dying wish to reunite us, and in some strange way reignite the town. So far Ashley and Morgan had done pretty well, restarting some of the old community traditions that had been slowly dying out.

"It's changed."

"It seems less magical somehow," Steve said, a strange longing in his voice. I wanted to peek at him but resisted. He'd lived in town for only a few years, having moved here when we were in the tenth grade. All the girls had been excited by his arrival. A new guy in a small town was pretty exciting for fifteen- and sixteen-year-old females.

Even I'd felt a little flutter the first time I'd met him, despite having just started dating Calvin. Because, really? Who wouldn't flutter? Steve was tall. Handsome. Smart. Someone new and different, with adventures from the outside world. Someone who would mysteriously vanish at lunchtime, never saying where he'd gone, just giving this slightly haunted, mysterious half smile when anyone asked.

Initially, I'd thought Steve was a nice guy, but the moment he'd seen Calvin slide his arm possessively across my shoulders, he'd turned opinionated about my life.

Complaisant.

There was nothing wrong with being agreeable. Nothing at all.

Unlike him. He thrived on chaos and frustrating people, which was so completely *not* what I was about.

I hovered at the top of the ladder, old anger burning through me and igniting old memories. With Steve feeding me the lights it had taken mere moments to get the length of them attached to the eaves. Now I'd reached out as far as I could, which meant it was time to scamper down again and shift the ladder.

As soon as my feet touched the snow, Steve was there, nudging me aside, with a "let me" as he moved the ladder over several feet before climbing it.

"I can do it," I protested.

He reached across the eaves, attaching the lights, his jacket rising above his belt, revealing what appeared to be a tanned midriff.

"Why are you tanned?" I blurted out. "It's December."

"I was in Morocco doing some volunteer work."

"Without your shirt on?"

He chuckled. "There are beaches there."

Why was my breath sticking in my lungs? He wasn't my type. I needed a guy who was content to curl up and watch movies through the winter nights, not go spend time on beautiful white sand beaches helping people.

Obviously, my priorities were way off when it came to men.

No, I reminded myself. Steve loved adventure. He was not someone a single mom could count on to be there. Not that we'd ever date. The first one to fall asleep would be murdered by the other, if our banter and digs from high school were any indicator. I'd loathed being his partner in chemistry, even though it had been outright freeing how I could speak to him, no holds barred. I could insult him and he'd laugh, somehow loving my moxie and the way I'd challenge him on things.

"What have you been up to?" he asked as he angled himself to climb down.

Not anything as cool as volunteering in foreign countries.

"I can do the lights," I said politely, reaching to steady the ladder as he descended.

"You still with Calvin?" he asked, his gaze fixed on the roof.

I sighed loudly and climbed the ladder as soon as he moved it. "Why? Are you looking to butt heads with him for old times' sake?" I glared down at him, but all he did was smirk. A smirk that would surely grow when he learned that our marriage—like he'd predicted—hadn't lasted.

Christmas Mountain was small, and I knew he'd have the answer soon enough. Like in about an hour, when Calvin came to pick up Max for their weekly "man dinner" with Calvin's dad. It usually involved steak at The Chop House, a hunting lodge style restaurant thick with leather upholstery.

"We separated last year," I admitted, then came down to move the ladder again. Why did it still hurt to say that out loud? We hadn't just separated. We were divorced. Officially.

Steve's calculating blue eyes met mine, and I lashed out, saying, "And are you still with any girl who'll smile at you?"

The way his lips danced with amusement while he looked at me in that direct way of his stole my breath. There was something about him that challenged me, made me feel alive, unhinged and... irritated.

I went to move the ladder, but he was holding it in place, still watching me with amusement.

"How's that fast lifestyle working for you?" I jerked the ladder from his loose grip.

"Fine. How's yours?"

"I *like* my life." I snatched the string of lights from his grip and stormed up the ladder.

"I'm sure you do," he replied mildly.

"I have the important things, and it's *rewarding*." A plastic clip for the lights broke, sending it flying into the snow. Wordlessly, Steve reached into the sack of extra clips hanging on the ladder, and seconds later handed me a new one.

"So is volunteering. You should try it."

"It's called my current job," I muttered, thinking of how Tonya had managed to snag more hours at Little Comets than I had over the holiday season.

"You volunteer? Where?"

"I was kidding. But I do volunteer at Max's school in—"

"Mom!" The panic in Max's voice made me clutch the ladder and snap my head in his direction.

"What's wrong?"

He was holding his green mittens under his bleeding nose. His gushing nose.

Lots of blood. And oh so red...

My head got light just like it had in biology class when I was seventeen. I clung to the ladder, trying to steady myself as I stumbled down the rungs.

"You're okay, Max," I said, trying to soothe him as my vision began to narrow, like headlights dimming on a dark winter's night as the battery began to die.

Not here. Not now. Not in front of Steve. And definitely not in front of Max.

"I've got you," Steve said, and I let out a breath of relief. At least someone could help my boy.

I jolted when Steve's large hands landed on my waist, before he helped me down the last step, then gently directed my head between my knees. I found myself almost wishing I would pass out so I could skip over this humiliating moment.

"You're okay," he said calmly. The presence of his hand on my back was soothing, and my vision slowly returned.

Obi was barking, jumping around us.

"It's okay, doggy. Yeah, just helping Joy," Steve said, his voice rich, calming. Obi-Wan pranced about, his tail whacking me in the leg, his nose nudging me at intervals.

"It's okay, Obi," I said. "You're okay, too, Max. Just keep holding your mitten to your nose. It'll stop soon."

"Hey, buddy, you got a tissue?" Steve asked Max.

"Mom! I'm going to bleed to death!" Max's voice was edged with hysteria and the dog left my side. I heard Max hit the snow with a "No, Obi-Wan Kenobi! No!"

"He senses a disturbance in the force," Steve said, his voice lifting in amusement at the dog's name. And he'd made a *Star Wars* reference. Max was going to love him. "He's using his Jedi skills to protect you."

"I don't like it!" Max yelled.

I scrambled to get the dog off him and the world swirled. Steve's grip on me tightened.

Why couldn't Max have his first real nosebleed on Calvin's watch? Or at school? Somewhere other than here and now?

I forced myself to stand upright so I could take charge. My vision was gray, but I could get Max to the house, pretend I was fine, then take it moment by moment. And not faint. Definitely not faint.

I took a few steps toward him, the tunnel vision returning. I bent over.

"Frosty punched me! He punched me and now I'm bleeding. I have to go to the hospital. Mom! *Mom!*" Max's voice was high, panicked.

"Let's get inside," Steve said in a soothing command. He'd left my side. "Keep your mitten against your nose. It'll all be okay. It's just a blood vessel that broke and it'll fix itself in seconds. These things are normal."

"But I'm bleeding!"

"Does it hurt?" Steve asked.

There was a pause as, keeping my head down, I groped my way toward the house, trying to act natural.

"No," Max said, his voice lifting with curiosity.

I needed to get over fainting at the sight of blood. It had completely derailed my life once, and now it was making it impossible to parent my own child when he needed me.

My vision fogged as I tried to head up the first step to the front door. Steve's arm hooked under mine, offering support when I wobbled.

It's just a nosebleed. Everything's okay.

My vision fogged even more.

I can handle this. It was nothing! Max is fine.

I stood up, determined to shut off this stupid physical reaction, but my vision went dangerously black. Steve practically lifted me up the steps as he said to Max, "Boots off. Then find some tissue in the bathroom."

He settled me on the bench at the door. Before he followed my son to the bathroom, he remarked, "So you're a mom?"

"Yes."

"And you never did become a doctor, huh?"

IN THE KITCHEN, I GAVE MYSELF A PEP TALK, HOPING TO GET RID OF that icky feeling in my gut. I hadn't passed out in front of Steve. That was a win.

From my spot I could hear Steve laughing at fart jokes with Max in the bathroom. Apparently males never outgrew the joy of body noises. Listening to them laugh shouldn't warm my heart, especially since Mr. Judgment was not only delighting my son, but had also saved the day.

But I was a mom—a single one at that—and seeing my son bond with an adult male was equivalent to an aphrodisiac. Anyone who could make my boy laugh and turn the tide on an upcoming freak-out earned a little heart thawing.

Even Steve Jorgensen.

There was a thump as small feet hit the bathroom floor, followed by a "There you go, buddy."

Moments later Max came ripping around the corner, his socks nearly sliding out from under him on the laminate flooring, his straight brown hair flopping to the side.

"Mom! Steve put a cold cloth on the back of my neck and pinched my nose and the nosebleed stopped! Did you know it was just broken blood inside me and that my body is already fixing itself?"

I smiled, remembering that exact same feeling of excitement and awe over the curious and very mysterious functioning of the human body.

"It's pretty cool, isn't it, sweetie?"

The sound of the washing machine lid clanging shut in the hallway outside the bedrooms, followed by a rush of water, took another thawing chunk out of the ice age-sized iceberg I held against Steve. He was washing everything that had been soiled so I wouldn't have to even see it.

If he wasn't careful he might meet Mrs. Sweet-and-Quiet, Gushing-Over-You Joy, and I had a feeling he preferred my tougher, let's-duke-it-out side.

"Steve knows fart and diarrhea jokes!" Max bounded over to the pantry door and flung it open. "Can I have the new cereal?"

"Sure."

"Really?" He eyed the clock on the oven's console. He knew it was getting close to suppertime. But honestly? Whatever. I felt gross, my body was still working through its own fight or flight —or play dead—chemical reaction to the nosebleed, and I didn't have it in me to argue nutrition with my son in front of Steve.

"Just this once."

"Best mom ever!" Max yelled, tucking into the task of dishing himself a snack.

Something cold hit the back of my neck and I flinched. I'd been ignoring Steve, focusing on Max, and hadn't noticed him approach with a wet facecloth, which he placed across the back of my neck.

"Do you have any hard candy?" he asked. He was standing close enough that I could feel the heat from his body.

"I have candy! Mom says I can have one piece a day. Can I have one now, Mom?"

"No."

"Your blood sugar likely plummeted," Steve said to me quietly. He was adjusting the cloth, and I wasn't sure if I liked the attention or not. Calvin and I had evolved into "just friends" during our marriage, and it had been a long time since a man had touched me. Not that Steve was crossing lines. But him being close, smelling like pine and fresh mountain air, somehow had my mind thinking about lines and what it would take to cross one.

"Can your mom have one of your candies?" Steve asked Max.

"She likes red. Do you want one, too? I have pink, red, blue and green. I ate the yellows and oranges. They're my favorites." Max had his bag of candy out, demonstrating his pure, generous spirit that made me love him all the more.

Steve unwrapped a red candy for me. "This'll get you feeling steadier."

"What are you, a doctor?" I asked, a tremor in my voice. He handed me the candy and I popped it in my mouth. It was so sweet it made my cheeks hurt as my salivary glands kicked in.

"Paramedic."

The usual sting of envy hit me in the chest at the medical career choice.

"I worked in some remote areas for oil companies. Texas, the UK, Canada, Australia, Saudi Arabia, Holland. You get bored, you move on. That's how it works." He gave me a smile that looked like it was supposed to reassure me of something. It didn't. It reminded me once again that he was still the same old guy he used to be. "I gave it up a year ago. You only need to see one major oil and gas disaster before you want out." He shrugged. "Now I fly helicopters."

Adventure. Move on when bored. I briefly teased myself with a quick visualization of what that life might feel like. Exhausting, no doubt. But a little bit cool.

"Jim Orson's looking for a new pilot for his business Rocky Mountain Helicopter Tours," I said.

Steve smiled.

Oh. He was Jim's new pilot. Of course. Steve was a man who answered the call of adventure even if it brought him back to this quiet mountain town.

"You're still really pale," he said. "How are your iron levels?"

"I'm fine." I took a deep inhalation, getting a lungful of his aftershave and outdoorsy scent.

"Pregnant?" he whispered.

I let out a bark of laughter so abrupt it hurt. He knew exactly why I had almost fainted, and yet here he was, poking and prodding at me and the one weakness that had changed my entire life.

Steve gave my shoulder a squeeze in support. I hated it. I loved it. Even though I was still wearing my down-filled jacket I could feel the heat from him like it had found a tunnel through the lining.

I glanced at him and realized with confusion that even though he'd never said a thing in high school, he knew. He knew what had happened on that fateful day in biology class. All it had taken to change my entire life plan was one scalpel. One thin cut into the amphibian victim, and I'd fainted like a lady-in-waiting whose corset had been done up too tight on a hot day.

Emma Winters had been freaking out when I'd come to in Steve's arms. Yes, he'd caught me, even though his station had been several over from ours. Because if you're going to humiliate yourself, you might as well go big.

I'd immediately begun crying and the teacher had ushered me out of class, assuming I was mortified—which I had been. But it was more than that. I knew that my dream was over. Through the years my tolerance for wounds of any kind had been slipping. And on that day, in Steve's arms, I realized I was never going to become a doctor, because doctors didn't faint when faced with the dissection of a frog. They also didn't get light-headed or dizzy at the sight or thought of blood, like I did. They waded through it all and saved lives without flinching.

Secretly, I'd spent the next several months trying anything and everything, from hypnotism and self-talk, to watching my hydration and blood sugar levels, to trying the Applied Tension Technique, as well as exposing myself to slasher movies with fake blood squirting everywhere—all in an attempt to alter the biology of my fight-or-flight reaction and save my dream career.

Nothing worked. If I saw blood or tried a dissection, I got woozy. Eventually I'd had no choice other than to throw in the towel, tip up my chin, block out the pain, and focus on what I had. Calvin. I slowly stopped talking about medical school, and when anyone asked about it I casually said I'd decided I'd rather start a family than spend the next decade in school.

I thought they would see right through me. But everyone had agreed, saying how much better it would be not to put that pressure on myself or take on the expense. Everyone except Steve, who had been unrelenting in his criticism for giving up on the one thing that would launch me out of this town and into a bigger life. Somehow he'd still believed in my dream—in me—and for some reason that had meant something that I still couldn't quite figure out.

"So you're a helicopter pilot?" I asked Steve, keeping my hands busy with wiping down the counter even though it didn't really need it.

"Cool!" Max exclaimed. "Do you do battle with starfighters?"

"No," Steve said, his lips twisting into a small smile. "I only take tourists out for rides or heli-skiing. No shooting. No leaving the solar system."

Max crossed his arms and gave a fake pout. "That sucks."

"Hey," I scolded.

"Nobody ever does anything cool."

This time Steve protested with a "Hey!"

Max swiped at his milk mustache from drinking the last of the liquid in his cereal bowl when I wasn't looking. He bounded up to Steve. "Want to see my *Star Wars* Lego collection?"

"Put your bowl in the dishwasher, please," I said. "And maybe later. I'm sure Steve has more unpacking to do. Moving is a big job. Remember?"

The sugar from the candy was helping me regain my equilibrium, and it was time to get Steve out of here so I could think.

"We moved here last year," Max informed him. "Mom and Dad each got their own house. I have two bedrooms!"

"Wow," Steve said.

I put a hand on his arm, happy there weren't sparks or anything electrical happening from touching him, as was often described in the books I read. He was just a man and I was just a woman, touching without sparks.

I guided him out of the kitchen and in the direction of the front door. "Thank you for your help."

He spotted the piano in my living room as we passed, and asked, "You still play?"

"Yes." Which reminded me I hadn't finished polishing its wood cabinet so the dry winter air wouldn't be so hard on it. The bottle of polish was sitting there, waiting for me. Just like the Christmas lights still dangling from my eaves.

"Cool." Steve stopped suddenly, looking me over. "Do you experience low blood pressure?"

"You can't fix me. I am the way I am, and I'm happy that way, too."

I knew where he was going to go next. He was going to try to find a solution. He was going to chide me for not trying harder, pushing further and becoming a doctor.

"What?" Steve gave me a quizzical look.

I quickly turned from the door to head to the kitchen. "Hang on a second. I have something for you."

"For me?" he said, surprise and hope lifting his voice. It made me wish I had something to bring him down—like hooking him to an anchor and dropping him into the ocean. I needed to set him in one spot and leave him there, because he was making me itch with the desire to complain how Tonya at Little Comets Daycare had taken one of my shifts again. I wasn't even half-time, with the latest reduction in hours. I kept telling myself it was cool, because we were both single moms, and she had more kids and less support from her ex.

But I had wanted those hours, and somehow just being around Steve was bringing that up, even though earlier I had been mostly fine with the arrangement. Now I wasn't. The way he could get under my skin meant trouble. Even the pig incident had been his fault. I would never have said yes to the idea if it hadn't been for Steve making me feel as though my life was boring and predictable.

And the shift at Little Comets? I didn't even need it. Calvin took good care of me and Max with his regular support checks, and my mortgage was small-town doable. It was just Steve getting in my head.

The plastic lid on the container of gingerbread men cracked as I opened it, then yanked several out for Steve. I hesitated, almost putting them in a plastic bag, until I changed my mind and piled them in a reusable container.

What was I doing? Now Steve would have to come over to return it. Or, more likely, I'd sit over here and fume, resentful when he didn't.

I stomped back to the front door. "Here." I thrust the cookies at his chest. How was a former paramedic who was now a pilot so buff, anyway?

And paramedic? He hadn't even been that great at biology.

"Thanks." His eyes lit up like they had when he'd opened his Secret Santa pocketknife. "I love cookies."

"We made them," Max said, dancing around Steve.

"Welcome to the neighborhood. And thanks. For everything."

Steve had slipped into his boots. They seemed so big compared to Max's, which were sitting next to his on the woven blue mat.

"So if you didn't become a doctor, what did you become?" he asked.

"I'm me. Like always." I gave a tight smile and said, "Congrats on your new job," while attempting to not slam the door behind him.

CHAPTER 2

"*W*ho is the long drink of water next door?" Cassandra McTavish asked from my front step. My friend was ogling Steve, who was doing something manly with power tools out on his driveway despite the flakes of snow drifting from the gray December sky.

I rolled my eyes. "Public enemy number one, so put your eyeballs back in your head and get in here."

Cassandra laughed. "Yeah, sure he is. He's making you want things, isn't he?" She waved her cowboy hat at Steve when he looked over, as though sensing he was being talked about. "Mmm. He's yummy."

I yanked her inside before she could cause trouble. Her four-year-old son, Dusty, followed her, saying, "The Joker is Batman's public enemy number one. He's the villain in Gotham City."

Max came running up, carrying a Batmobile toy in each hand and passing one to Dusty. The two boys raced off to play, Max loving the feeling of being like a big brother to the younger Dusty.

"Thanks for letting us stop by," Cassandra said, hanging her thick farm coat at the door. "Dusty's been going stir-crazy. Sometimes I wonder why we live way out on the ranch. Although I'm sure Alexa will remind me of all the reasons why when she arrives for Christmas. However, Texas doesn't have winter the way we do, which automatically makes it easier."

"Your sister is coming?"

"Yup, and her hubby, Cash."

"They're both coming?" I'd heard how difficult it was to slip away for a holiday when you had a ranch to take care of.

"Yup! Her new hired hand, Nick Wylder, and his girlfriend, Polly, have been great. Alexa actually booked a full week away. I'm hoping she'll want a working vacation, though." She flashed a smile. "I could use her expertise."

Cassandra had grown up on the ranch she now lived on, having gone to school one town over from Christmas Mountain. Cassandra, from what I'd pieced together, had left the ranch years ago for the East Coast, where she'd gotten married and had Dusty. Her sister had come for a visit to help Cassandra through her difficult pregnancy, but had stayed on when Cass's marriage to Dusty's father dissolved in a hot mess. Alexa had found work as an executive assistant during that time, and on a quick trip to Indigo Bay with her boss, had fallen in love with him. The rest was history, with the two of them ending up on a Texas ranch, and Cassandra back on the family ranch in Montana. I had the feeling that Cass missed her sister more than she let on.

"Do you think you'll ever return to the East Coast?" I asked, leading her through the living room and past the partial wall that sectioned off the kitchen. I turned on the coffeemaker and leaned against the counter.

"Montana's still home," she said with a sigh. "But sometimes I wonder what I'm doing as a single woman on Blueberry Springs Ranch. I'll never find a man out in the boondocks, and there's no way I'm dating the help."

"Men just complicate things," I said.

"What's wrong with you and Calvin?" my friend asked, her expression turning to one of concern.

"Nothing."

"Or did you find a new man?" She perked up. I shook my head and she shifted back to the topic of Calvin. "Is he still talking about Paris?"

"They leave in two days," I said, careful to keep my voice steady as I fiddled with the sugar bowl. Max was tagging along to check out France with Calvin. They were making an official vacation of it, with a planned stop at Disneyland Paris, as well. The two were going to bond even more deeply, which had always been a secret wish of mine. And yet, I had reservations, too, like I feared being replaced in Max's heart.

"I still can't believe you guys might move," Cassandra said.

If Calvin liked what he saw in France, and thought he could contribute to some big project, he was moving, and we would follow.

"You don't want to go, do you?" my friend asked gently.

"Oh," I said, waving my hand. "You know me. I'm happy in Christmas Mountain, but family comes first. I'm sure France would be an incredible experience for Max."

"So, tell me about your new neighbor." Cassandra leaned forward with a grin. She'd had a nasty divorce when Dusty was still a toddler, but she didn't seem to be turned off by the idea of finding someone new—or someone new for me, either.

I brought the empty cups and sugar to the table and sat across from her, pushing her favorite mug her way. It had a sunset ocean scene from the time I went to California for a long weekend with Calvin.

For a moment I allowed myself to imagine finding love again. I adore Hallmark movies, where the characters always get swept up in a sweet love, and the complications in their lives just sort of resolve themselves and fall away. Was real love like that? Kind of like what Calvin and I started out with, but with some staying power and a lot more of a kick?

I sighed. Calvin and I had never seemed to quite find that spark I saw in the movies. Maybe because we'd been so young. Maybe because I wasn't adventurous, but rather a happy wallflower. Or maybe because movies were fictional feel-good dreams and not reality.

Either way, I had the feeling that men liked women who were more lively and spontaneous than me. Someone they wouldn't lose interest in over the long haul.

"What's that scowl for?" Cassandra asked.

I smoothed my features. "What scowl?"

"You could find someone, you know."

"I have Max." I wished the coffee was ready so I could pour it while smoothly changing the subject.

"He's going to grow up and leave one day. Then what?"

The idea caused a pang in my gut. Max was only seven, but I already dreaded the day he'd move out. When he'd first started spending time at Calvin's last winter during our separation, I'd nearly died of loneliness. Hence the dog.

"He's going to Paris for a week with his father," Cassandra pointed out. Another pang, this one bigger. "What if they move there?" These pangs were starting to cause an ache.

"I already told you I'll go, too."

Cassandra sat back, watching me with serious eyes that had seen more than her fair share of hardship.

"How about you?" I pressed. "Are you ready to climb back on the dating horse?"

"Nope." She got up and retrieved the insulated carafe even though the coffee was still mid-brew. "Not yet."

"Two divorcées," I teased, trying to hide my smug smile. "Sad and alone."

She pointed a finger at me. "I will not be alone forever. I *am* going to get back out there. I'll find a man, and when I do, I'm going to make him mine."

"Why am I picturing bondage against his will?" I said, feigning concern. "How much rope do you have on that ranch of yours anyway, cowgirl?"

Cassandra snorted before letting out a laugh that rang loud and true.

The front door opened and a woman called out, "I hope you guys didn't start without me."

"I'm just nagging Joy to speak up for what she wants," Cassandra yelled back, sloshing dark liquid into the red-and-white cup that Max had painted for me last Mother's Day—a thoughtful gift arranged by his teacher. "Perfect timing, Carol!"

"Joy, listen to Cassandra," Carol Bennett ordered, followed by the resounding thunk of snow boots hitting the mat at the door. "Who is that hottie next door? Is he the reason for this conversation about speaking up for what you want?"

I choked on a fake laugh.

Carol and I went back as far as elementary school and Melody King's choir group. We'd both left Christmas Mountain after high school and hadn't kept in touch. But once Ms. King fell ill last year we'd found our way home again, along with the other gals, and had since all reconnected as though no time had been lost.

"Because I can see why you'd want him," Carol said, entering the room while unwinding a long, rose-colored scarf that brought out the cheerful highlights in her hair. "So if you're trying to summon the courage to request some adult time with him, I totally back up Cass."

"It's about Paris. She doesn't want to go," Cassandra said. "But I agree about the man, too."

"I said I'll go to France."

"And isn't the neighbor lovely?" Cassandra continued,

ignoring me. "He's that perfect blend of big but not bulky, you know?"

"You don't want to go to Paris? I thought you were gung-ho to experience a different culture with Max?" Carol asked, handing me a book from her store, Rudolph's Reads. Pretty much every business in town had a Christmas-themed name, and hers was no exception. "You'll like this one. It's an autobiography about a woman who changes her entire life after divorce, and basically goes out and kicks butt."

"Inspiration for us, perhaps?" Cassandra asked, snagging the book from me to read the dust jacket. "Did she move to Paris to follow her ex?"

"I'm not *following* him. It'll be an enriching experience for all of us—if he takes the job." For Carol's benefit I added, "And that's Steve Jorgensen living next door."

Carol recoiled. "No." She stared at me like I was making stuff up.

"Yes," I said reluctantly.

She began laughing. "I assumed my eyes were lying and that it couldn't be him. I mean... next door? To you?" She laughed again. "How is he even still alive? If you need help hiding his body, I've been eavesdropping on the mystery novel book club that meets in my shop, and I might have a few suggestions."

"It's not that bad having him as a neighbor," I muttered into my cup. Maybe the spats that Steve and I had had were more legendary than I'd realized.

Cassandra was grinning at me as if I'd revealed something juicy.

"Have you told him today how awful he is?" Carol teased.

"Of course I have." I tucked my shoulder-length hair behind my ears. Technically, I hadn't told him that. But since our meeting last night was less than twenty-four hours in the past, I figured that counted.

For Cassandra's benefit, Carol pointed at me and added, "This crazy woman used to pick on him *every day* in school."

"I did not," I mumbled. "And he started it."

Carol took the bookworm mug I'd won in a raffle last year and filled it, putting the carafe back in the machine as she told Cassandra the full story. "Steve moved to our school in tenth grade and every single girl had a crush on him. He was hot. Smart. Intriguing. Adventurous. Total catch. But this girl—" she waved her hand "—made him her enemy." Carol turned back to me. "So? Is he single? Has he asked you out yet?"

"Why would he do that?"

"He's always had this protective vibe around you, like he was some sort of Neanderthal who wanted to drag you back to his cave and kiss you."

I rolled my eyes, trying to ignore the shivers that zipped through my body at the thought of Steve kissing me. I'd bet his kisses were divine.

Except for the whole it-being-Steve thing. I shook off the fantasy. "You need to get out more. And read fewer caveman romance novels."

"That's not a genre," Carol protested. "But it should be."

"I bet it is," Cassandra said.

"Remind me to look that up if I forget."

"The only thing that Steve has for me," I said, "is picking apart my life and making me feel like I'm not living up to my potential. And that wanting a family is boring. He acts like his life goals are superior." The heat of anger had returned. He'd really managed to get under my skin all those years ago, and had gotten me all riled up again yesterday, as though I'd never moved past it.

Carol waved away my argument. "You're single. And I heard from Jim Orson that Steve is, too."

"Plus, he has a point," Cassandra said. "There *is* more to life than simply raising our sweet little hellions."

"And there are also several good reasons why Steve is still

single," I stated, locking my hands around my cup. His personality being the key one.

"But he's hot," Carol said, sighing wistfully. Cassandra smiled and gave a low hum of agreement.

"*So?*" I pressed.

"And he's smart." Carol lifted a brow. "You like smart. Does he read? I'm a sucker for a reader."

"He's bossy," I countered. "He thinks he has the right to dictate what I do with my life."

"Just like Calvin," Cassandra muttered, as Carol scrunched her nose.

"We *discuss* things," I argued. Calvin had a say in my life, but he didn't run the entire show.

"I never saw that side of Steve," Carol said. "I only saw the two of you flirting—sorry, verbally attacking each other—in class."

"Has he really made you feel less than worthy again?" Cassandra asked, tipping her head to the side and sending her curls into a tangle.

"Well..." I fumbled for something concrete to support my claims. "He..." He had been nothing short of awesome yesterday. But I knew what he was like, deep down. I knew what his judgment felt like, and that if I waited long enough it would pop up and blindside me.

"Why should I like Steve?" I asked in a defensive tone, more than a little curious about what they'd heard about him.

"He carried Mom inside when she fainted," Max called from the hall outside his room, "and he fixed my nosebleed."

The little eavesdropper. Seriously. Heat was already creeping up my face as I tried to figure out how to explain the incident, while my friends gaped at me in surprise.

"It wasn't like that," I said numbly.

"You were holding out on us?" Cassandra gave me an unimpressed look, her hands flat on the table, her shoulders hunched forward as if she was preparing to lunge at me.

"It's the quiet ones you have to watch out for," Carol said knowingly. She had leaned back, legs crossed, her coffee mug secured between her elegant hands.

"He didn't carry me."

"Wait," said Carol slowly. "Do you still have that thing about seeing blood?"

"What thing?" Cassandra asked, looking at me.

"I tend to get woozy when I see blood, even though everything's totally fine." I closed my eyes, trying not to picture Max's mittens clutching his nose.

"It's why she didn't become a doctor," Carol said.

My eyes flew open. "You know about that?"

She shrugged. "I figured it out a few years ago. At first I thought dissecting the frog was an isolated incident. Because you were still totally fascinated and dived right back into the project the next day—as long as you didn't have to dissect." She turned to Cassandra. "Steve caught her when she fainted in class."

"No," Cassandra breathed.

"Yes. I thought she was finally going to see Steve's attention for what it really was, and date him instead of Calvin."

"Wh-what?" I sputtered. "I don't like Steve. I have *never* liked him."

"So he had to carry you yesterday?" Cassandra asked. "Like, to your room?" She had a funny expression on her face, and one hand tucked under her chin.

"I just leaned on him, and then he put a wet cloth on the back of my neck and gave me a candy to bring my blood sugar back up." I began talking faster, worried they would believe the whole situation had actually meant something. Which it hadn't. But it felt like it could if I wasn't careful. "He ran all of Max's things through the wash after getting him cleaned up."

Realizing I was twisting a tendril of hair around my finger, I dropped my hands to the tabletop and locked them around my cup once again.

Cassandra had a far-off expression that probably wasn't too different from my own. Single moms have two kinds of fantasies. The first I call Hot Men Scenarios. They're the standard sweep-you-up, real-life-doesn't-exist ones. And then there are Thoughtful Hot Men Fantasies, where the guy runs loads of laundry while cleaning the entire house and making you dinner. Preferably something gourmet.

Both are enough to send a woman off to la-la land for considerable amounts of time.

"You have a crush!" Carol giggled.

That broke the little fantasy playing out where Steve was wrangling with Max's mattress, getting the fitted sheet on in such a way that a bouncing boy couldn't pull it off simply by bounding into bed each night.

"I do not."

"So totally do," Cassandra said with a small smile. "And who can blame you?" She sat straighter and took a sip of her coffee. "Maybe I'll have to develop a fainting condition, too."

I gave an exasperated, humored sigh just as someone knocked on the front door. It swung open and a male voice called out, "Knock, knock! Just returning your cookie container."

STEVE MADE HIMSELF AT HOME IN MY KITCHEN IN NO TIME, Cassandra cheerfully offering to pour him a cup of coffee while he protested that he could serve himself. I noticed he chose the largest cup in the cupboard—a big polka-dotted mug I'd been given by one of the daycare kids last week.

Max shot in to give Steve a quick hi, and Steve gave him a fist bump while taking a gulp of his freshly poured coffee. I hated the way the little moment made my heart swell.

"Carol!" My son turned to her next. "Do you have any new

books about galaxies? I want to read about Tatooine! It's where Luke Skywalker is from."

I'd recently done a little shopping in Carol's store while she kept Max entertained with a book about outer space. He was eager to go back and fill in the gaps in his knowledge.

"Tatooine is a fictional planet, Max," I said. "It's not real."

"I know," he told me, his focus on Carol.

She hummed thoughtfully, and I wondered if she was plotting how to sneak more books under our tree from Auntie Carol. "There are a lot of interesting books about *Star Wars*, and I have a new shipment coming this week. I'll text your mom if there's anything good in there, okay?"

"Okay! Thanks!" He scooted off to go play again, hollering, "Dusty! I'm getting new *Star Wars* books!"

I sighed and winced at Carol, who just laughed and told me not to worry about it. She turned her attention to Steve. "Long time no see." She held out her hand. "Carol Bennett. We were in the same grade."

"Yeah, I remember. How's it going?" Steve shook her hand and took the empty chair next to me.

"Emma says hi, by the way," I interrupted.

"To me?" he asked.

"No, to Carol."

"She was the cute one, wasn't she?" Steve's focus was soft, as if he was trying to conjure up a mental picture of Emma.

My eyes narrowed involuntarily as an unwanted sting of jealousy hit home.

"I heard you're a helicopter pilot?" Carol asked Steve.

"I am."

"But he doesn't fight with starfighters," my son interjected from the other room. "He stays in this galaxy."

"Thanks, Max!" Carol called. "I was wondering about that."

"What have you ladies been up to?" Steve asked. His cup had

paused in front of his lips, making me notice how entirely kissable they were.

My friends were getting in my head. I was *not* interested in him.

"I'm Cassandra." She reached out to shake Steve's hand from her spot across from him.

"I'm sorry. I should have introduced you," I said.

"In case you need a quick catch-up," Carol said, "Cassandra runs her old family ranch, I own Rudolph's Reads here in town, and Joy works in the daycare down the street."

"You do?" Steve asked, glancing at me. It was a curious look, not yet judgmental, but I figured all he needed was time. Because once he thought about it, he'd realize I had taken a job that didn't pay well, needed very little training, held no prestige, no benefits, and was in the same small town I'd grown up in.

I waited. The judgment didn't seem to be coming.

Realizing Steve was waiting for confirmation, I nodded.

"Full-time?" he asked, his attention as focused as the unrelenting summer sun.

I shook my head. "Half-time." I accepted almost all shifts offered by Edith, but still couldn't get myself over the hump to full-time.

"Does Max go there, too?"

I shook my head again. "He's in school now."

"You're going to ask to get closer to full-time, though, right?" Carol pressed.

"Edith had to make additional cuts." I sounded more glum than I meant to, and quickly put on a smile before my friends started to worry. "It's fine, though. Tonya really needed the extra hours this month. She doesn't get much in the way of child support, and Calvin takes good care of Max and me." Anyway, the daycare couldn't afford to hire us both full-time due to the increase in benefits they'd be required to pay. Plus there weren't enough kids in town to support a large staff.

"That boy is going to grow up one day," Cassandra muttered in warning, before taking another sip of her coffee.

"I heard you went to college," Steve said, leaning an elbow on the table.

"I took a few early childhood education classes." Calvin had insisted I take some courses toward at least a diploma, so I'd have something to fall back on. I'd helped him get his degree by working reception at a car dealership while raising our son, but by the time Calvin finished school I was tired of being broke all the time, and had wanted to spend more time with Max. Calvin hadn't been excited about me quitting, but he'd understood why I hadn't wanted to pursue a full diploma or degree, and he'd seemed happy enough about no longer having childcare costs as I'd stayed home until Max entered school.

"So you have a teaching degree?" Steve asked, his face lit up in a way that made me want to say yes.

I shook my head and the excitement faded. I turned away before I could see that disappointed look I had grown to know so well in high school.

"Do you ever think about expanding your career?"

And there it was. Being a daycare worker wasn't enough for him.

Carol gave me a smile and raised her eyebrows.

I shot her a questioning look.

"You should upgrade your education!" she agreed, laying her palms on the tabletop. "Say goodbye to that daycare."

Being a teacher would be great, but it would take a lot of time and focus, as well as money—things I didn't feel I had right now.

"Goodbye to changing diapers and wiping drool," Cassandra exclaimed.

"Goodbye to poor hours," Carol added.

"The schedule is good. I need that flexibility," I insisted.

"Poor pay," Cassandra said.

"Max is in school full-time now," Carol pointed out, seamlessly defeating my argument.

"I like being able to go volunteer in his class." My voice faded as I realized my excuse was actually more ammunition for them.

"You could be getting paid for what you do in the classroom," Cassandra stated firmly.

My friends nodded, watching me.

I leaned back, surprised by their encouragement. Didn't they know things were okay with me working at the daycare—other than Steve stirring up a desire to want more? A dangerous, slippery slope any way you looked at it. And sure, being a teacher would be incredible, but I couldn't afford to go back to school for several more years, or to uproot Max's life as I returned to the city to study. He was my priority right now. He needed stability.

"She is *so* awesome with the little ones," Carol said to Steve. "Very patient and understanding." Her attention went back to me. "You'd be amazing as a teacher."

"You should do it," Cassandra insisted. "Forget depending on Calvin. Make something of your own."

"I bet your courses could be applied toward a teaching degree," Steve said. "That would cut down on time and cost."

"I like the way you think," Cassandra declared, high-fiving him.

Carol propped her elbows on the table, looking thoughtful.

They were planning a new career for me. And here I'd been worried they were going to try to set me up with Steve.

"Working at the daycare is fine," I argued, standing up. I went to collect cups, but everyone was still sipping away. They weren't even ready for a top-up. I sat down again. "It's rewarding."

"It's not fine," Carol said quietly. "You're stressed about money and hours."

"I'm not."

"You might be able to take some of the courses online," Steve suggested.

"I know a guy in admissions at the college in the city. I'll ask." Carol pulled out her phone and began tapping out a message.

"Ask how much she can do off-campus," Steve told her. Carol nodded and continued to type.

"Do you have to do a practicum?" Cassandra asked.

"Mrs. Rogers at the elementary school takes education students all the time," Carol said, not looking up from her phone. "She'd take Joy in a heartbeat. She's always talking about how much her daughter, Anya, loves her."

"Really, I'm sure I can look all of this up—*if* I become interested. You don't need to bother your friend, or Emily Rogers." I really wanted to pull Carol's phone from her grip and hide it from her.

"She won't look it up," Cassandra whispered, reaching out to tap the table in front of Carol. "Send the message."

I heard the telltale sound of a text being sent.

"Seriously, you guys." I laughed nervously. "I like my job. I'm not going back to school."

"You'd love it, and you'd have the same holidays as Max," Cassandra pointed out. "Add in benefits and health insurance, maybe even a pension... That's huge. You aren't getting that right now, and as a single mom you have to look out for number one."

Everyone nodded.

The security was tempting.

"I'm too quiet. I couldn't control a classroom." It would be so much work, juggling classes, lesson plans, and taking care of Max, too. I wasn't sure I could do that.

"You're awesome with kids!" Cassandra practically shouted. "You can get those little turkeys at the daycare to line up like a bunch of penguins. Not just anyone can do that." She said in an aside to Steve, "I can do it with horses. But kids? Forget about it."

Carol jerked her head emphatically. "You come alive with kids, my friend. I saw you patiently coaching those tykes how to snowshoe. They had so much fun I heard about it down at

Prancer's." Prancer's Pancake House was the hotbed of local gossip, and I was pleased to learn I was making waves down there for good reasons.

"The kids make it easy," I said modestly.

"*You* make it easy."

"You know we're right," Steve interjected smoothly, a slightly smug smile in place.

I fought the urge to glare at him. Somehow this was all his fault.

"I couldn't control a whole classroom full of kids," I said firmly, wishing they'd let it go so I could at least give the idea some consideration without feeling the need to defend myself.

"You keep telling yourself that," Cassandra answered. "Just keep lying to yourself all day long."

"Lying is bad!" Max called.

Seriously. Would that kid ever stop listening in on my conversations with others?

"You can step onstage and play the piano for an entire community," Steve said gently. "I'm pretty sure you could get up in front of a bunch of kids Max's age."

I chewed on my bottom lip. I did love volunteering in his class, and it was often the highlight of my week. But the tuition and time to get trained as a teacher...? The city was a long drive from Christmas Mountain, and who knew if there'd even be a job opening when I graduated?

"Performing is different," I said, backtracking. When I played for an audience the piano was like a shield. It wasn't me everyone was focusing on, it was the music pouring through the instrument.

"She teaches piano lessons," Carol said. "She's already teaching."

"Oh!" I said. "Speaking of pianos, does anyone know of a local tuner? The one who tuned mine after we moved cost me an arm and a leg."

"Must be difficult playing now," Steve said drily, earning a chuckle from Cassandra.

"Wise guy," she murmured with a smile that made me want to push her away from him.

"Are you trying to change the subject?" Carol scolded, looking at me.

"The Christmas Extravaganza is coming up, and the community center's piano is horribly out of tune after being moved around all year because everyone kept bickering over how best to renovate and restore the building's interior. You guys won't be able to sing on key if I can't play on key."

"You still perform in the extravaganza?" Steve asked, perking up. He was leaning his arms on the table, relaxed, looking like he belonged here.

Carol nodded. "We started up again last year."

Our little choir group had taken a hiatus for eight years, but we were reviving the tradition. We'd started in the sixth grade and continued until graduation. This would be our first year performing without Melody King as our leader, and it was something I tried hard to avoid thinking about.

"Are you going to come?" Carol asked Steve, and Cassandra gave me a grin. I found myself looking to him, waiting for an answer.

He shrugged and nodded. "Probably."

During my years away I'd missed the sense of community from the town's holiday celebrations, and the concert always brought up good memories. But a confusing one, too, as I recalled seeing Steve standing against the back wall of the old church watching me play the piano. He'd had a look on his face that I still couldn't quite figure out all these years later. I was curious if I'd see that expression again this year.

"I can tune a piano," he stated, breaking the silence that had descended.

We all faced him.

"What?" I asked softly.

"I rented a room from a piano tuner when I was taking my paramedic courses. I can probably get it sounding okay if it's not too far out of whack."

"You're hired," Carol exclaimed. She dug around in her jeans pocket. "In fact, I happen to have the key for the community center right here. I was there dropping off decorations. I'll let Michelle Millar know Joy has the key. Feel free to tune it at your leisure. Although, just make sure you get the key back to our darling caretaker by five tonight, as she needs to let Ashley and Brent in to change some light bulbs."

I took the Santa keychain and handed it to Steve.

He shook his head. "I need someone to come with me."

"Why? You've forgotten where the community center is?"

"No," he said slowly. "So that someone can tell me if my tuning is up to her specifications." He took my hand, and a sharp zing waltzed its way up my arm from his touch. The key was still in my palm and he folded my fingers around it.

What was with the zing? That was offside, unfair and unwanted. That was *not* how Steve and I worked.

"That's not how you tune a piano," I said, feeling a bit breathless.

"I'm not an expert. I also don't play piano. Just guitar."

Why did I have a mental image of the two of us playing a tune together in my living room, laughing, smiling and sharing a moment?

I shook off the thought. He'd probably learned just a few bars from "Stairway to Heaven" to impress a chick, and now told everyone he could play.

"It would cost hundreds to bring a professional in—if we could even get someone before the concert," Carol said, her voice holding a touch of warning. "So I guess you guys better go down there. Together."

"Now?" I balked, tugging my coffee cup closer as though it could protect me from time alone with Mr. Bossy Pants.

"Now," Carol confirmed.

"We'll babysit," Cassandra offered.

"We only have the key until five," Carol said, taking charge. "And I know nothing about pianos. It's up to you two."

"We can borrow it another day. I'm sure Steve is—"

"No time like the present," he interrupted, standing up. "Jim warned me the holidays tend to get busier with tourists wanting helicopter rides, so we may as well get to it." He gave me a quick nod.

"Always the bossy pants," I grumbled as he ushered me to the door with a warm hand against my lower back. But for some odd reason I didn't mind his touch or insistence nearly as much as I believed I should.

CHAPTER 3

*T*he silence was awkward as Steve and I cut down Star Street, across Main and over to Church Street. The Christmas Mountain Community Center, converted from an old church, was only a four-minute walk from my house, but it felt like a decade. It didn't help that Steve seemed content to walk in silence.

When we started out I'd asked him if he wanted to grab his tools for tuning the piano, and he'd patted his pocket and announced that he was all set. I was starting to get the feeling he didn't know how to do the job, given that his so-called tool kit could be tucked in his pocket rather than being large enough to resemble a doctor's bag.

"Here we are," I said, trying to be cheerful as we approached the back door of the center. Thanks to the hard work of a community painting bee last summer that was led by some of my favorite gals—the old choir group—the converted church looked a little less abandoned than it had a year ago. The exterior white paint was fresh and bright, making the historic building look majestic with its mountain backdrop, and I inhaled the aroma of home. Snow and evergreens. And something new and equally wonderful.

With a jolt I realized the new olfactory delight was Steve.

The steps were still cracked and iffy in places, and we carefully chose our route as we climbed toward the door. I let us into the darkened building, light sifting through the windows in faded streams. Partially blind from being out in the bright sunshine which had been reflecting off the snowdrifts, I fumbled forward, trying to recall just how far down the wall the light switches were. I bumped into something solid. Steve.

He mumbled an apology and pressed a hand to my back as he reached around me, hitting the lights, which flickered a few times before illuminating the large room. I was partly trapped between him and the wall, and found myself curious about who Steve really was. The one thing I'd learned in the daycare was that everyone behaved the way they did for a reason. Everyone had a story and a history, even if they were only a few years old. And that story impacted their choices and the way they behaved. I knew that held true for Steve, a man who'd moved here as a teen, then left, like me. And now he was back. Like me.

But why? Why here? And why now?

"How long are you here for this time, Steve?" I could see my breath in the chilly air of the building, which was kept at a low temperature to avoid running up a high heating bill when empty.

Steve still hadn't stepped away from me. He was watching me, his eyes meeting mine. "As long as I'm wanted."

By who?

"And then where will you go?" I asked, curious if he had family drawing him somewhere, like my family had drawn me back to Christmas Mountain.

He shrugged. "We'll see. How are your parents?"

"Still the happiest married couple I've ever met."

He chuckled. "Why do you say that with disgust?"

"There's no disgust."

"There definitely is."

"Okay," I admitted with a sigh, as he moved toward the piano at last. "Maybe there is a little bit. But seriously? Are they faking being that much in love? They make it look easy."

Steve cast me a glance over his shoulder. "Maybe if you find the right person it *is* that easy."

"And what would either of us know about that?" I asked with a laugh. The nice thing about Steve was that I never worried about hurting his feelings.

The piano, an old upright, was on the stage, and I dropped down on its dusty bench, sloughing off my gloves, then mindlessly running my fingers up and down the keys, which had been left uncovered. There was a definite vibration on Middle C that shouldn't be there.

"Maybe we just need to open our minds," Steve said, lifting the stiff lid to the piano's cabinet.

"To what? Possibilities? I am not going to date Old Man MacLeod. He gives every woman who passes the hairy eyeball, but that is not an invitation I plan on ever accepting." I gave a fake shudder.

Steve laughed. "That guy's still around? He must be in his hundreds by now." He took out his phone and used its flashlight app to peer inside the piano. He gave a whistle.

"What?"

"There are a lot of strings in here."

"Do you know what you're doing?" I asked, hitting a few keys.

"Ouch! Stop that."

"Sorry." I sat on my hands, so I wouldn't be tempted to knock his fingers a few more times. All eighty-eight keys were covered in a layer of grime from a year of disuse. Off to the right I could see a D key that wasn't sitting properly. This thing was about trashed. Bringing it up to a reasonable standard was going to take not only time, but skill—something I was certain Steve was bluffing about possessing.

"There's a high D looking odd. How does it look in there?" I asked.

"Which one's odd?"

"Are your fingers clear?"

"Yes."

I popped my head up to peek at him. He was doing something on his phone instead of looking inside the instrument.

"What are you doing? Researching how to tune a piano or texting your girlfriend?"

He gave me a saucy glance, and I couldn't decide whether that meant yes, he was researching the job, or no, he was texting some woman.

I tapped and wiggled the funny key, which remained silent. I needed that one for "I'll Be Home for Christmas." We planned to play it in honor of Ms. King this year. I just hoped we didn't choke up for sentimental reasons. "What's up with this key?"

He bent forward again. "Wire broke. We can probably bring it back to life if we use a little care. Bring out this old beast's potential."

"I don't know if it can be salvaged," I said, taking in its condition again. As a kid it had simply been a piano. You sat down, you played your music, you got up again. But looking at it now, with its chipped and yellowed keys, I realized the past few years of neglect and abuse were certainly showing, and I didn't believe it was up to the task of making up for any faults us gals had in our singing or playing. It was time to have the instrument replaced.

Steve was watching me over the top of the cabinet. "What are you saying?"

"I'm not sure yet." Replacing a piano wasn't easy when money was tight. Could we squeeze another season out of it?

He closed the lid, then set a very familiar looking pocketknife on top, which sent a surge of adrenaline through me. He still had the knife? I met his gaze, but his eyes didn't give anything away. Maybe it wasn't special to him. Maybe it was just something handy, like a keychain, that he didn't even think about. And of course, the gift had been a secret. He didn't know the pocketknife was from me, but for some stupid reason I wanted him to.

"We need to find you a new piano. Where should we start looking?"

"I didn't say it needs replacing right now," I said, frustrated by his take-charge demeanor. "Quit trying to solve problems that aren't yours."

He met my eyes, a thread of history dangling between us, tangling the past with the present. I found myself wishing he would back off and let everything be. Life had felt simpler before he'd moved in next door. I knew that his helpful actions didn't warrant my frustration, but it was Steve. I never seemed to be able to act truly reasonable around him.

"This will do for another year. It just needs tuning." I ran my fingers down the out-of-tune keys again, hitting the dead one and leaving a hole in the sound ringing through the empty building.

Steve eased away from the piano, hands raised in surrender. "Just trying to be helpful..."

There was something in his steady, even gaze that made me uncomfortable. It wasn't anything I'd ever seen from Calvin, and I wasn't sure what it was. It was like Steve was considering me, trying to see what was behind my need to argue with him instead of simply placating me and carrying on with his plans.

It left me feeling exposed.

"Don't tell me what I need in my life," I said, glancing down as I played the scales.

He stepped to the piano, casually leaning against it, a lock of hair falling across his forehead. "You need something?"

"No. And this piano is good enough. A new one would need tuning after being delivered, anyway." I stood up, shutting the piano cover. "So maybe you should just tune it like you said you would." That would at least get us through this year. The building needed a roof more than a piano, and eventually the fundraising group would be able to replace it.

"Maybe," he said, taking a step closer, "despite how you try to convince yourself, it's not good enough."

"And maybe you don't know everything," I challenged with a glare, daring him to glance away. The fiery look I sent him was returned with a gentle, understanding one that made me feel like a broken, wounded animal lashing out due to pain.

I was *not* a wounded animal.

"Maybe you should stop accepting things that you shouldn't," he said.

"The piano is fine, Steve." I was calm now. That weird place between emotions. "Maybe you should accept that not everything needs changing just because you want it to be different."

He came around the piano, and for a moment I feared he was going to tenderly cup my chin and kiss my forehead. Or lips.

"Maybe you need to learn to speak up," he said. "Demand more. Reach out and grab what you want in life."

"Fine," I said, the word coming out more breathless and less firm than I'd intended. "Bring me a glorious new piano, Steve, or fulfill your promise and make this thing work again. And while you're at it, how about finding me a job that pays better, too?"

I clamped my mouth shut.

He smiled knowingly, which angered me.

"Quit trying to mess up my life, Steve. I'm happy!"

"Follow your dreams, Joy. Follow the yellow brick road," he crooned.

"Maybe this *is* my dream." I crossed my arms, my insides trembling.

I was a single mom working in a job that would never allow me to fully pay my bills without Calvin's support. How could *that* be my dream?

"Maybe there's room for more."

"Like a teaching certificate." I jutted out one hip, daring him to confirm that he thought I should pursue something that would break my bank account.

He shrugged, not saying a thing, which made me want to fight even more.

"Going back to school sounds so fun. I'd be pinched for time, traveling to the city, almost four hours away—if not actually moving Max there after finally settling him here, or even worse, leaving him behind and becoming a long-distance mom. A busy, distracted, stressed mother, as well as in debt. Sounds like I'll provide Max the kind of childhood everyone dreams of. And for what? The possibility that I might be able to teach a classroom full of kids and financially support the two of us?"

"Sometimes we have to make minor sacrifices in order to—"

"You're not a parent. You don't understand."

"Enlighten me."

"Try listening!"

"You see the problems, but what about the other things? The rewards?" I shut my eyes, fighting for control as he continued. "Financial security. Sharing the same holidays as your son. Using that amazing brain of yours."

I opened my eyes to lash out as his tone became soft, but he was reaching for me as if he planned to stroke my hair. I tipped my head away, confused by his tender expression. His fingers missed their intended mark, and he grasped a tendril of hair, stepping closer to delicately tuck it behind my ear. The unexpectedness of his actions made me quake, dissolving the anger and filling me with something else. Something I couldn't identify. I didn't like it. It made me feel vulnerable and uncertain.

I was pretty sure it was longing, but didn't know if it was for his touch or for the career and lifestyle he'd described.

"Maybe you need to learn to be happy with what you have," I whispered, unable to take a step back despite my desire to.

"I'm trying. I keep failing at it." His lips had twisted into a wry smile, his gaze displaying that same tenderness I'd felt in his earlier touch.

"Well, maybe I already reached out to get what I want. I have a home. A son. A job. A car. I don't need more."

"Did you pick them all out yourself?"

I opened my mouth, then closed it before saying diplomatically, "Calvin and I decide on these things together. As a couple. That's what we do."

Okay, so the cute little cottage-style home I'd selected in the historic section of town after our breakup was vetoed by Calvin because its insulation—a must for mountain winters—wasn't as good as the home he'd selected for me. And yes, he'd also convinced me that my all-wheel drive SUV was better than the cute sedan I'd been leaning toward. But I had gotten to veto the bungalow he'd chosen for himself, as well as the bigger SUV he'd thought I'd like. He knew me well, and neither of us had given up our autonomy by listening to each other.

"Why are you so bossy?" I asked Steve, my tone revealing a hint of disgust.

"Because I'm good at it."

"Expert level," I muttered, turning away to sweep a palm through the dust gathered on the piano top, then smacking my hands together to clean them.

"Are you going to look into becoming a teacher?" he asked.

"Why can't you understand that I'm fine working in a daycare?"

"Because you're not."

"Haven't you been listening?"

He watched me for a second while I battled my feelings.

"You're a good liar," he said gently.

I gasped with indignation. "I am *not* lying. I like working there." Which was true. The hours and pay just weren't enough to keep me going.

"Don't be afraid to change your life."

Tears welled in my eyes. "I'm not afraid of change."

Paris. Paris was a change—a big one. What if it happened?

But I wasn't afraid. I wasn't. I just didn't want all the upheaval. It felt like we'd just gotten settled, and Max was just getting used to his parents living in separate homes and in a small town instead of the city.

"Look," I said, clearing my throat. "I have paint to pick up from the hardware store. So if you're done pretending you know how to tune a piano, can we go?"

"Paint?"

"Max wants a blue bedroom." I gestured toward the door. "I'm going to surprise him."

Steve nodded slowly, moving toward the exit, one eye on me. I could feel his judgment washing over me, seeping between the cracks.

"You know, not everyone likes to just waltz off on adventures, with no cares or responsibilities," I said, my tone a bit preachy. "Maybe some of us like having a stable life and don't need more. We don't need to disrupt our lives due to some insatiable thirst for action and excitement. Maybe I just need a job, and a home and Saturday movie night with my son. Maybe that's the important stuff." I turned at the door and locked eyes on Steve. "You know—family."

Steve's stance softened, as did the look in his eyes. "You're right."

His words took the fight out of me, as did the pang of loss in his gaze.

We climbed down the steps in silence, finding the snowy, sunny world too bright after being inside. I felt riled up, angry, sad and frustrated. Typical emotions after spending time with Steve.

"I do know what it's like to have responsibilities," he said quietly, taking my elbow when I skidded on an icy patch.

"Thanks."

"And to have someone depending on you."

I stopped walking. "You have kids?"

He stopped, too, his gaze averted to the evergreens lining the road. "My mom was sick when I was in high school. I went home at lunch to make us a meal, and to feed her before coming back to school again."

"I'm sorry. I didn't know."

He finally looked at me, his contemplative expression making his eyes seem a shade darker. "You have an amazing son who seems very well adjusted. That isn't easy."

"It is easy. Calvin and I get along very well."

"I know." He reached out, gently stroking his thumb against my chin just once while he repeated, "I know."

THE WALK BACK TO MY HOUSE WAS FAST—TOO FAST. WE WERE AS silent as we'd been on the way over to the center, but my mind was a mass of confusion, and I didn't know what to think or what to say.

There had been something in Steve's expression that just...

He couldn't be envious of Calvin.

Calvin didn't even love me. When we'd broken up he'd said he didn't believe we'd ever really been in love. That alone had blind-sided me.

He'd said we'd been too young, and what had we known about love?

The fact was my own husband of seven years and five months hadn't loved me. The only man I'd ever been with hadn't ever truly fallen all the way in love with me. The father of my son.

It had felt like it should have been love.

And then there was Steve... He was like one of those chocolate eggs that Max loved. You never knew what was hidden inside, sometimes a toy, sometimes a puzzle.

Steve was the puzzle when I'd been expecting a toy.

He pushed me and made me think when I didn't want to. But maybe it wasn't for the reasons I'd always assumed. And then when he was pushing me, and I was about to snap, he would drop back and do something unexpected.

It was infuriating, and I found myself wishing that he was more like Calvin—straightforward and easy to predict. Other than the no-love bit, Calvin was linear, like a marble rolling down a tube. Steve, on the other hand, was a bouncy ball operating under zero gravity.

I turned to face him at the bottom of my steps, the yard's inflatable Frosty bobbing jovially as the fan at his base kept him plump with air. Steve had walked me to the door even though he could see me from his place and it was still daylight. Maybe he was hoping for a second cup of coffee with the gals.

So much for my must-go-buy-paint excuse. I had a houseful of friends waiting for me to return home.

"Why have you never liked Calvin?" I asked.

"What does a new piano cost?" he asked at the same time.

"What?" It took me a moment to catch up with him. "I'll hire a real tuner. One who has tools and isn't overwhelmed by the number of strings inside."

"Funny." He smirked, not at all put off by my dig. "So seriously. How much?"

"I asked you a question."

"I asked one, too. How much?"

"A lot."

"How much was yours?"

"A lot."

"You're in a real helpful mood, aren't you?"

I put my hands on my hips and swiveled to face him more fully. "I wasn't expecting tuning the piano to be such an issue."

"So? It is. Let's solve it. We could restore it, but we don't have a ton of time."

"The piano isn't my problem." I waved toward the community center and sighed.

"If you plan on playing music for the extravaganza, then it *is* your problem."

I was tempted to roll my eyes, but refrained. The crunch of tires on the packed snow indicated I had company. I bit my top lip as I recognized the SUV. It was Calvin. I wasn't sure if I should appreciate his timing or not.

"Man-night steakfest was yesterday," I said, as soon as my ex stepped foot on the walkway. He came to a halt and stared at Steve and me.

"What do you need?" I asked, feeling impatient with his unexpected visit.

Calvin was wearing a fine wool coat, his black loafers shining against the white snow. Straight from work. Mr. Handsome Engineer. It wouldn't be long before he started dating again, I realized. The man was a catch—just not mine—and I was certain women weren't leaving him alone.

"I thought we could discuss some last-minute details about Paris," he said, his gaze fixed solidly on Steve.

"You're going to Paris?" Steve asked me, his voice laced with disbelief. "With him?"

"Calvin and Max are going." I gave Steve a look as if to say "butt out." Not that he was ever very good at that, but it would be a lovely Christmas miracle if he figured out how to do it, starting this instant.

"He's taking Max?" Steve asked, his brows raised as if he found the idea incredulous.

Yes, my little boy was going to be gone during the lead-up to my favorite holiday—one that just wouldn't have as much joy in it without him asking me about Santa and his reindeer, while crossing the dates off his calendar. But this trip wasn't about me. It was about Max and his dad having an experience neither

Calvin nor I had ever had. There would be plenty more Christmases.

"Steve Jorgensen," Calvin said, his tone flat. "You're back in town."

Steve stood a bit taller. "Living right next door." That smile sure seemed smug.

Calvin took a long look at me, then shifted his attention back to Steve. His jaw was tight, like the time Max spilled grape juice on our new couch. "Of course you are."

"Indeed I am. And you're still... you."

How had he made that sound like such an insult?

"Max has a playdate and the ladies are over," I said, moving toward the steps again. The men taking licks at each other now that they were adults felt wrong. We should all be past this—even though I didn't seem to be.

"What are you two doing out here?" Calvin asked. He'd come closer to me, his eyes still on Steve.

"Talking." I crossed my arms, then softened my stance when Calvin gave me a slightly wounded look. We didn't shut each other out. It wasn't how we worked. We were a team. One with communication skills, not resentment or fights. "We were checking out the piano at the community center."

"Joy believes it's had its season," Steve said. He eyed Calvin's Buick SUV. It was freshly washed and looking shiny and perfect. "I was thinking I'd scour the used ads, but maybe you'd care to donate one? Your wife sure could use it for The Christmas Extravaganza."

I shot Steve a look while Calvin crossed his arms, his chest puffed out.

"He can't afford another piano," I muttered. Louder, I added, "I need to check in with the gals."

I turned, about to climb the steps, when Steve muttered back, "Spent it all on the Buick, huh?"

"You need a piano, honey?" Calvin slid his arm across my

shoulders, placing his hip against mine and preventing me from escaping inside. My heart lifted at the endearment, even though I knew it meant nothing. "Why didn't you say something? I bet the engineering company I work for would be more than happy to donate one. And if not, maybe I can find one like I did for your living room." He shot Steve a smug look.

"You'll find one?" I turned in his half embrace. It was familiar, warm, but somehow didn't feel as right as it once had. "You leave the day after tomorrow. I'm going to need the piano right after you get back, and it'll have to be tuned after being delivered."

"I can tune it," Steve interjected.

"By a professional," I added, not even turning to him.

Calvin let out a huff of amusement, his features relaxing as he slipped his arm off my shoulders. "You two still hate each other, huh?" he said.

"We don't hate each other," I answered lamely, taking a step away.

"Hey! Look who's here," Carol called from the doorway. "I thought I heard voices. How's the piano?"

Obi came trundling down the steps to circle the men before sitting at my feet, then stretching to nudge Steve's hand, hoping for a few pets, which he was granted.

Calvin whistled for the dog and was ignored.

"The piano's fine," I told Carol, worried that my stubbornness was going to land us in hot water when it came time to perform for the town on a piano that sounded awful.

"Joy won't say it, but she feels it could use replacing," Steve interjected, giving me a hard look. "She's too forgiving. She could do a lot better than settle."

I narrowed my eyes at him.

"But don't worry," he said brightly. "Wonder boy here says he'll get one." He jerked a thumb in Calvin's direction.

"Really?" Carol's forehead furrowed.

"I'll look into getting something brought in," Calvin said smoothly.

"Aren't you leaving for France?" she asked.

"I've got this," Calvin assured us.

"I'm going to go next door," Steve said. He reached out and tapped my shoulder. "Open your window and holler if you need anything." He smiled and winked, while giving Obi-Wan a goodbye scratch.

I rolled onto the balls of my feet, trying to think of a reason for him to stay longer. I didn't have one.

"She won't need you," Calvin said tightly, his hands curling into fists. "She has me."

I turned to him in surprise. And that's when I saw exactly why the two men had never gotten along.

"It doesn't make sense," I told Cassandra, ten minutes after Steve had left, followed soon after by Calvin and Carol.

"It makes total sense," my friend replied, palms flat on the kitchen table. "Calvin's jealous of Steve and vice versa."

"I know. But it still doesn't make sense."

"Steve has a thing for you, which is driving Calvin nuts."

"But Calvin doesn't want me."

"That doesn't mean he wants his old rival to win you. And why else would Steve pretend he can tune a piano except for the fact that he likes you?" Cassandra laughed, having loved the story of Steve's moxie, going all the way to the church and never quite admitting he was in over his head.

"He would do all of that to annoy me," I said.

"It's only annoying because you like him, but don't want to." She smiled as if she'd hit upon some truth—which she hadn't.

Steve and me? We were like ketchup on pudding. It just didn't work.

"He's annoying because he's still pushy and thinks he knows what's best for me. He intentionally made Calvin jump up and say he'd get a piano."

"Well, the one at the center *is* old. And it's not like Calvin is broke. Steve probably did you and the community a favor." Cassandra moved toward the front door, hollering for Dusty, who had finished helping Max clean up the toys they'd been playing with. We were in that precious, momentary balance where it was imperative to extract the boys before the mess was recreated.

"And," she added, reaching for the door even though her son was still in Max's room, and by the sounds of it, trying to see who could jump the highest on the bed, "I also happen to agree with Steve that you should become a teacher."

I gave her an unimpressed look.

"It'll only take a few courses, right?"

I folded my arms across my chest and she lowered her voice, adding, "Max really likes him and so does Obi."

"So?"

She raised her brows, calling me on my feigned obtuseness. We both recognized that Steve was hitting some pretty important marks on the single mom's potential-new-husband list. Good with your kid? Check. The dog likes him? Another check. He had earned himself a free pass straight into the inner circle, where his eligibility could be considered more fully. Because chances were he was a good person.

"He likes a life full of adventure," I said. "He's not looking to play daddy."

Cassandra smirked, and I paused, wondering why my excuse felt like a lie. Was it the way Steve softened when I'd talked about family when we were in the old church?

If I was a decent judge of character—and I liked to think that I was—it seemed as though he might actually *want* a cozy family life.

I shook my head. That didn't line up with the Steve I knew. He was a helicopter pilot dropping people out onto glaciers and snowy ridge tops so they could ski their way down to the bottom. If that didn't say adventure, nothing did.

Cassandra hollered for Dusty again. "Come on, kid! Tim Burke is waiting for us to pick up that saddle blanket for the community center's silent auction. If we're going to help put a new roof on the place we need to get moving. Chop, chop!" She lowered her voice again. "By the way, Tim's a rancher in need of a woman." She fanned herself. "Totally cute. As for Steve, why don't you kiss him and see if all this fighting is just chemistry with nowhere to go?"

I gave a huff of amusement as Dusty came sliding up in his socks. Cassandra plunked a red knitted hat on his curls as he jumped into his boots, and she had him out the door in moments, adding, "Be like Nike. Just do it."

I waved goodbye and closed the door, to find Max already in front of the TV, clicking through the channels.

"Did I say yes to screen time?"

"Yup."

"I didn't. Turn it off."

"But I'm tired and want to watch."

"Why don't you finish your letter to Santa so I can mail it? That way it'll get to him in time for Christmas."

"Santa!" Max bounded off the couch and into the kitchen, yanking his half-written Santa letter from the fridge and sending the magnet flying. As nice as the upcoming break would be, I was going to miss my little whirlwind.

Just pretend he's going to be over at Calvin's for a week and not half a world away.

I sighed and held up the list of things to pack for Max that Calvin had left with me. It was long, but I could see at a glance it was missing important items, such as Max's favorite teddy bear. I tossed the list aside, wondering what Calvin would do if I ignored it.

Right. He'd be steamed up, because it was me who took care of the details, desperately hanging on to my little boy and the idea of being needed.

What had changed that I didn't want to deal with packing? Was it a belligerent part of me that thought if Calvin was going to take our son on this international trip, then he was on his own and could very well mess up and fail? Did I want the vacation to be miserable for poor Max? Because that's what could happen if I didn't add items to that list. What a corner I'd painted myself into.

"How do you spell 'Mercedes'?" Max asked.

"You don't need a car," I replied absently, picking up Calvin's list again.

"Dad wants it."

"He already has a fancy car." Because he made more money than a daycare worker did. Because he'd taken care of himself by getting a degree, instead of quitting like I had and then just floating along, assuming he'd always be there. And now he wasn't.

He had the nice car. I had an okay car, which I was grateful for. I plunked myself down at the table and shoved my hands in my hair. I was a grown-up, and couldn't afford the same things my former partner could, even though we'd been hip to hip all our adult life. What kind of spot had I inadvertently put myself in?

Steve was correct, as were my friends. Going back to school would be smart. But was it the right choice?

And was Calvin really going to find me a piano? I shook my head at how Steve had played to Calvin's weaknesses—or jealousy, according to Cassandra—causing him to step up in the piano-replacing department when it was the last thing he had time for.

As if on cue, my phone beeped with a text from Calvin, saying there were no used pianos online in the area, and that maybe the fundraising group for the community center could sort something out in time.

I put my phone down, wanting to ghost him by not replying. Instead, I picked it up again and sent him a thumbs-up emoji, hating the way I was letting him off the hook, but very aware that I was preventing a fight, which was probably what Steve had been angling to create.

I shifted my chair closer to Max's, hands clutched around my phone as I reminded him to put spaces between his words so Santa could read the letter easier. I wondered what Steve had asked for from Santa at this age. And how was it that none of us had known his mother was sick? And why did that tidbit of history feel connected to the way he'd judged me and my life choices in high school?

Had I messed up in my assessment of him? But why had he judged me for wanting to start a family with Calvin, when today his eyes had softened when talking about family?

Had he changed?

No. He was still pushy, as well as correct about most things in my life, from my career to the community center needing a new piano. The worst part was that if I did go through with upgrading my education, it would be due to him, and a part of me didn't want to give him the satisfaction of being right or thinking he knew me.

I thought about texting Carol to see if she'd heard back from her friend in admissions, but instead I set my phone down. It was time to focus on my little boy, not on the hunky man next door who was trying to turn my quiet life upside down.

CHAPTER 4

I kept waving even after my father-in-law turned the corner, taking Max and Calvin to the airport, along with Calvin's mom. Finally, I lowered my arm, letting my shoulders sag. I swiped at my eyes with my middle fingers, frustrated that my plan of wearing non-waterproof mascara hadn't worked to keep my tears at bay.

Obi nudged my thigh with his nose as I sniffled.

"I know," I said, my voice embarrassingly wobbly. The temptation to shove items into a suitcase and follow Max to the airport was far too great.

I would not follow them. I no longer belonged with Calvin, and we were no longer a family unit. Calvin's mother was going on the reconnaissance trip to act as chief caregiver for Max when Calvin had meetings. Not me. As Cassandra had said, Max and Calvin wouldn't always be front and center in my life, and in this moment the fact had never felt so real.

I needed to stand on my own two feet, starting right now. I stared at my house, the urge to make an instant move down the path to significant life changes itching like mad. I still hadn't heard back from Carol about admissions to the education program, and until I knew more about going back to school I didn't want to tease or tempt myself with dreams of a career change.

Forcing my feet to move, I headed back toward the warm house, my breath coming out in clouds in the frigid morning mountain air. Inside, I kicked off my boots and stared at the black TV screen in the living room.

Tonight was movie night. I dropped heavily onto the couch. Max and I hadn't missed a movie night together since we'd moved in a year ago.

A small squeak escaped me. No. No feeling sorry for myself. This was an opportunity for both of us. Max would gain some independence, while seeing more of the world, and I would watch something rated higher than PG tonight. I could curl up in bed with a glass of wine and a movie, or I could eat junk food on the couch. I could turn the music up too loud.

I nodded to myself, feeling bolstered. But then my head began shaking slowly. The house was too quiet. Too... dull and lifeless. I got up and plugged in the Christmas tree. Pretty. I waited for the spirit of the holidays to envelop me with its warmth. Instead, the cold reality of loneliness crept in.

This was exactly what Cassandra had been warning me about.

Outside. I needed to go outside.

I hustled to the door and pulled on my winter gear. A walk would clear my mind and help me find a much-needed Zen head space.

"Walkies!" I called to Obi, and he came scurrying around the corner, his nails clacking on the floor.

I clipped his leash to his collar and in moments we were out in the sunshine as it crested the mountains, highlighting the entire town with a magical, early morning glow. I hurried down the steps and hung a right, planning to start at Christmas Falls, then maybe take one of the trails out into the bush beyond the Kissing Bench.

I passed the community center, wondering once again what I was going to do about the piano. The extravaganza was coming up fast, all seven of us ready to perform, whether we had an instrument or not. But if we didn't have a piano what would I do? I wasn't much of a singer and didn't want to be left out of the group. We'd all met up at the tree lighting ceremony last week and had shared cookies baked by Ashley's mom, like old times. It had felt good, real. Laughter, connection. I didn't want to lose that even if I didn't wear Ms. King's friendship bracelet every single day, like I had for the tree lighting ceremony.

Huffing and puffing from my frantic pace, I took the steps up the slope to the waterfall, and drew up short in front of the Sharing Tree. It was covered with ornaments, as per the community tradition. Word was that if a couple hung an ornament on the Douglas fir together they would be lovers for life. Calvin and I had purchased an ornament for the occasion back in our last year of high school. We'd planned on hanging it, but when I'd opened the box in front of the tree, the ornament had been broken.

A bad omen? Coincidence? Bad luck? I didn't want to consider what might have happened if we'd managed to hang the ornament.

Instead, we'd kissed at the falls on Christmas Eve, and as per local lore, we'd had good luck for a wedding in the New Year.

I nearly laughed at my thoughts, and continued past the tree. It didn't matter. It was just a wish. A tradition. Not at all real.

There was someone on the path ahead of me, and I called Obi back as he bounded over to the familiar-looking hiker. I called out an apology and the figure turned. It was Steve. My heart gave a little skip, but I wasn't sure if it was due to anticipation or dread.

"Hey, Joy."

"Hey."

"You saw your little guy off okay?"

I bit my cheek, trying to trap the sudden welling of emotion so I wouldn't start blubbering like a fool. I sufficed with a short nod.

France was so far away. And Max would be gone for so long. We'd never been this far apart, or for so much time.

Wordlessly, Steve came over and rested a hand on my shoulder. The unexpected empathy made my eyes fill with tears. I was still wearing that crappy mascara and I shifted away, desperate to regain control.

"I guess it'll give you some peace and quiet so you can apply for college, huh?"

There was a twinkle of amusement in Steve's eyes as I retaliated for that barb, giving him a playful shove. His feet slipped on the packed snow and, horrified, I reached out to catch him. My hands slid around his waist, so I was pressed to him as he continued to wobble. We were going to fall. His arms clenched tight around me as we struggled for balance. Then he righted himself with a chuckle, causing me to realize he'd never been in real danger of falling.

"Seriously?" I gave him a glare as I dropped my arms. But I was still locked in his embrace, Obi dancing around us, barking happily.

"It's been some time since a beautiful woman wrapped her arms around me." He was giving me a lovely hug, his puffy down jacket like a pillow. I loved it. I hated it.

"What are you doing up here?" I choked out, feeling as though I'd given up something by letting him hug me. "Adding an ornament to the tree with your invisible girlfriend?"

"Something like that."

I watched him for a moment, his gold-flecked blue eyes studying mine.

"What?" he asked, that crooked smile dropping.

I shrugged, suddenly unsure as he released me.

He looked as though he was going to say something else, then changed his mind.

"What?" I echoed. This was becoming awkward fast. And since things with Steve never got awkward, this was new ground. I didn't like it.

"Want to walk with me?" he asked, the awkwardness vanishing as quickly as it had appeared. He held out his hand, offering assistance down a particularly slippery part of the trail that was sheltered by trees.

"Okay." I let my gloved hand slide into his, tempted to fake slipping so I could land in his arms.

How mixed up was I that his embrace seemed like the best part of my day?

We headed on down, his hand dropping mine where the trail narrowed, this route less traveled than the one leading up to the waterfall. Obi-Wan loped ahead of us, his fringed tail making happy circles in the air.

"Steve?" I ventured at last.

"Yeah?" He took a look at me over his shoulder and I was hit by the directness of his gaze. He was so handsome, so kind. And he took the crap I blasted at him and somehow knocked me sideways with it, then righted me once again.

I shook my head, unable to summon the courage to say what was on my mind. "Nothing."

"What?"

"It'll sound bad," I admitted.

"I don't mind bad."

"I know." It was one of the reasons I liked him. "I just wanted to say thanks."

"For what?" He turned to look over his shoulder again.

"For letting me knock you around with my words."

He stopped so suddenly I almost walked into him. I halted in turn, standing too close, and stumbled back a step. Steve's brow was deeply furrowed, as if I'd just told him the world was in danger of being hit by a meteor.

"You don't knock me around."

"I know. You're tough. But sometimes I come close, and I hope you know it's not personal—not really. It never has been."

"Okay."

"It's just that when I'm with you I..." I floundered, unable to explain what I called the Steve Effect. Somehow, I became someone else when we bantered. I was free to be bold, fully honest, with nothing held back. Free to explore my thoughts and feelings without worrying about reining myself in.

"When you're with me... You're you," he said simply, breaking into a wide, warm smile.

I nodded, wishing he'd hug me again.

"Steve?"

"Yeah?"

"Do you want to be my friend?"

Steve had given me a small smile as he'd nodded, accepting my invitation.

He was my *friend*.

The word felt foreign and novel in this context.

We were home now, shifting shyly on the sidewalk in front of my house, unsure what to say. I released Obi, who shot off into the backyard.

"Thanks for preventing the bears from eating me out there," Steve said, filling the silence that was stretching between us.

"They're all hibernating." I hesitated. "Is your mom..." The words trailed off. I was suddenly greedy to learn about Steve and his family life, but felt it was too soon to dig in. I wanted to know everything, from how he was spending Christmas to what he'd bought as gifts for his relatives. Even what holiday traditions he liked and looked forward to. "Sorry, it's none of my business."

"I thought we were *friends*," he said, his voice that lovely, gravelly baritone.

"I know, but..." I was smiling now, unable to stop, but I felt bashful. Almost like a teenager with a crush.

"Is she still alive, you mean?" Steve's words were carefully chosen, and I knew she hadn't won her fight with the sickness he'd mentioned the other day. "Unfortunately, she passed away."

"I'm so sorry."

He reached out, tapped the back of my hand. "My life can be your business, Joy."

"Sorry, I just..."

"What?"

"It feels like this could be a no-go area."

He stepped a little closer, peering at me. "It's not. I'm an open book."

I didn't reply, and he said, "Ask me anything."

I narrowed my eyes as though about to analyze the truth of his upcoming response. "Do you really know how to tune a piano?"

Steve tipped his head back with a joyful chuckle, then focused on me with a smile that made my chest feel tight with emotion. We were connecting. *Friends*.

"I've had the best online video teacher there is," he announced.

"I like your confidence. I hope Max grows up to be..."

Steve considered me. "Would it be so bad if he turned out like me?"

"I don't particularly want to fight with him all the time."

"So? Then don't fight with me." Steve angled closer, his feet bracketing my own. My breathing slowed as I attempted to anticipate his next move. It felt like it might be a kiss.

He brushed back a strand of hair that wasn't tucked under my hat.

"But that's what we do," I said, my voice embarrassingly breathy. "We fight."

"It's not a rule."

"It isn't?"

"No, it's not." His voice was low, confiding. His lips were close to my own, the warmth from our breath battling the cold air that surrounded us. "And we don't fight. We challenge each other."

My heart was thrumming loudly in my ears as I dared to look up, to meet his steady gaze while still firmly planted in his personal space. It felt like I was facing down something huge, taking a massive step into the unknown just by looking at him this way.

"I think we're going to make great friends," he said. His hands brushed the sides of my arms, his mouth still angled like it might land on mine sometime soon.

My nerves got the best of me and I laughed.

"You don't want to be my friend?" He was still close, but leaning away now.

"No," I said quickly.

His smile fell.

I realized with terror that I might want more than that. More than friendship.

"What?"

"I want to be friends, but we... we had a love-hate relationship in high school," I said quickly. "But without the love part. Can we actually not kill each other?" My laugh was fake, awful. "Because this—" I pointed to the narrow space between us "—is feeling like we're missing a pretty big step, and you should know that I'm done with love and relationships and everything else." I swallowed the large lump forming in my throat, hating the hollow feeling that had developed inside me. I couldn't even look at Steve, because I felt foolish. I wanted him to kiss me. I wanted to get swept up in the moment even though I knew he would become bored with me, leave me, break my heart.

And possibly Max's, too.

Steve's hands cupped my face and I jolted, but when he didn't advance, didn't move or speak, I looked up.

"Take a breath."

"I am!" I wasn't. I was freaking out.

"Learn this, okay? Love alone isn't enough to bring happiness," he said. "You need more than that. We all do." His gaze lowered as he licked his lips. "I think you're awesome. And yes, I would have loved to kiss you a moment ago."

My mouth dropped open as I started to retort. Before I could he placed a gloved finger over my lips. "But more than that, I would love to be your friend."

The fight in me waned, and as something within me softened, Steve pulled me into his arms.

"I'm sorry that your love for Calvin wasn't returned in the way you wanted." His voice was tender, making tears pool beneath my closed lashes. "Everyone deserves to be loved back, with just as much oomph as they feel."

The tears broke free as well as a hiccupy sound. I was still wearing that poor excuse for mascara and I raised my hands to wipe my eyes, causing him to release me before I was truly ready. How was it that two little conversations with Steve did more damage to my makeup than saying goodbye to Max?

Steve pulled a clean tissue from his coat pocket, drying my cheeks.

"Where was that tissue when Max had his nosebleed?" I muttered, trying to regain control of my emotions.

Steve chuckled, then shrugged. "I decided it would be smart to keep a couple stashed in my pocket. I do have a rather active seven-year-old living next door. And his mom, as you may have heard, could use a little help when he gets nosebleeds."

He gently wiped away the last tear, and in his open expression I saw so much honesty and caring that it was all I could do not to launch myself into his arms again.

"Thank you."

"You're welcome." He wadded the damp tissue into a ball, as if he wasn't sure what to do with his hands. "What are you up to next?"

"It's movie night tonight," I said, the quaver in my voice betraying me.

"Already, huh?"

When I nodded, he caught my head in his hands, tipping it down so he could place a kiss on top of my hat. He took a few steps backward and I longed to follow him.

"Thanks for the walk," he said, giving me a small wave.

I watched him stride away, feeling more let down than I knew I should.

I STOOD ON THE SIDEWALK FOR A LONG MOMENT, WATCHING STEVE head into his house, before I went into mine, feeling oddly rejected. Somehow he had broken me down, making me feel both vulnerable and connected, and then had just turned and left.

Why would I ever think Steve Jorgensen could be the man I needed? He wasn't equipped to handle weepy women or lonely moms, and I was currently both.

I threw my winter wear across the room in frustration. Obi chased down my striped hat, retrieving it with enthusiasm. Rubbing his ears, I sighed and told him he was a good dog, then took my slobbery hat and tossed it into the wicker basket under the bench at the door.

Why had I exposed myself to Steve? And why had I taken the almost-kiss and made it into a big deal, followed by a grand shutdown? Maybe he hadn't actually planned on kissing me. Although he'd said he wanted to.

I leaned against the door and touched my lips, curious how it would feel. Would he be tender? Or would kissing him bring some crazy sparks to life, like in a romance?

He'd said he was an open book, but I had become one. I'd laid it all out there like I was desperate for his validation or something.

I grumbled in frustration and faced the empty house. Now what? I couldn't start watching movies at noon. Not that I really wanted to. Maybe I could pretend it wasn't Saturday—that movie nights didn't exist when Max was away. Even though Calvin and I shared our son, with a week on and a week off, Calvin always got him for man night and I always got him for movie night.

I didn't have any piano lessons to prep or teach again until January, but I had presents that I could wrap as a distraction. I could also get lost in the memoir from Carol for a few hours. But instead of heading to my bookcase or digging out my wrapping paper, I sat down at my old laptop, waiting while it whirled and hummed, struggling to get me online.

If I was going to go back to school I would need to upgrade my computer. Plus teachers were expected to do some work from home, and so much of it was computer-based these days.

I pushed my chair away from the table. What was I thinking? Was I serious about becoming a teacher?

Spinning in my seat, I faced the pale yellow room.

What if Calvin said yes to the job in France? How could I work on getting a degree if I followed him to keep our family close? Instead of going to the college website like I'd planned, I closed the laptop and leaned back in my chair, feeling deflated.

I flipped over my phone, seeing a text from Carol. Her friend in admissions had said that if I applied before his holidays started on Tuesday, I'd know before January if I'd been accepted and whether they could fit me into the program. As well, he'd mentioned that the first four classes toward my degree could be taken online, and that I might qualify for some scholarships.

It seemed so possible to go back to school, and yet not quite possible, either. I set my phone down and moved to the piano, breathing in the familiar smell of freshly applied polish. I lifted the lid and ran my fingers lightly over the keys. This old friend could get me through any funk, and I was certain that once I finished playing I'd have the answer on what to do about my future.

As my fingers struck the first chords of "O Come All Ye Faithful" my mind snapped out of thinking mode. I became one with the music, the energy and peacefulness of the carol flowing through me.

I felt a smile tug at my lips as I swayed, becoming my own metronome to keep the beat.

Song after song, I played through the afternoon, until the early dusk of the mountain town settled in around me. The muscles between my shoulders had grown tight and I rounded my back, stretching them out. I was ravenous, but my mind was blessedly blank. Everything that wasn't about this moment could wait for another day.

I ran my fingers noiselessly over the keys in a silent thank-you before closing the lid, staying there for several more moments.

I was lonely. Not fully satisfied with where my life path had taken me. I had so much to be grateful for, but I had also led myself into a corner, my future not quite as open and full of opportunity as I'd once expected it to be. Calvin was treating Max to a trip to France, a day at Disneyland Paris, a week of eating out and staying in hotels, and I was at home counting my pennies. I had definitely gone wrong somewhere, but it wasn't entirely too late to remedy that.

Before I changed my mind, I opened my laptop and began filling out an application to enroll in one of the larger state colleges—the one where Carol's friend worked. Several minutes later I hit Submit and sat back, hands shaking.

I'd done it. I'd applied to go back to school.

I reminded myself that I didn't have to say yes if they accepted me; I was simply opening doors for myself, to see what might come through them.

The doorbell rang, sending Obi into a flurry of barking, and making me jump. I shut the lid of my laptop and peered through the peephole before opening the front door.

"I ate the last gingerbread man," Steve said, stepping past me, a shopping bag nestled in his arms.

"You already brought back my container."

"Hey, pup." He bent to ruffle the long fur on Obi's back, making the dog grin. Then he tipped his shopping bag my way so I could peek inside. Popcorn. Candy. Drinks. "I thought maybe you could use some company for movie night."

My heart soared and I threw my arms around Steve, giving him a giant hug and crinkling the bag.

"I think I'm going to like movie night," he said, wrapping his free arm around my waist. "What else happens? Any kissing?" He waggled his eyebrows, and I burst out laughing despite how only hours earlier I'd called us out on the whole skip-a-step thing we seemed ready to perform with an unprecedented leap from enemies to almost-kissing. There was something about this crazy man that could make such chagrin-inducing moments laughable. It was as if, when I thought my whole world was about to fall apart or get complicated, he simply walked through the door and opened every window and shutter, letting in sunshine and making everything feel right once again.

"What?" he asked. "You have a funny look on your face."

"I'm thinking."

"You're not thinking about kissing, though," he mused. "Your expression isn't dreamy enough."

"I keep catching myself liking you."

"Well, you should like your *friends*. And shouldn't that be a dreamy look if you *like* me?"

"How's this?" I clamped my hands together under my chin and batted my lashes.

"Remind me again why I agreed to be your friend?"

"You're funny, Steve. Cocky, but funny. And you need someone to keep you in line. I'm that gal."

"I prefer the term *confident*."

He set down the bag of snacks and unlaced his boots. I took his coat, even though there was a hook for it right beside him. The coat was surprisingly thick and weighty unlike most of the newer designs. I bet it felt good, secure, all snug around his torso. Kind of like how his hugs made me feel.

He handed me the snack bag and I nosed through the contents. "What's the tablet for?"

"I have some movies on it. You probably have something picked out already, though?"

"Are you trying to curb your bossiness?"

He smiled. "How am I doing?"

"Not bad. Even though you did invite yourself over."

He paused, his boot halfway off his foot. He caught my smile and gave a small shake of his head, knocking the boot the rest of the way off.

We made popcorn in the microwave and opened the cans of iced tea, and since the couch was definitely the best seat in the house, we both sat on it, at opposite ends, neither of us even considering the love seat. Progress in the friend department?

"So? What are we watching?" he asked.

"Well," I said slowly, "I usually choose a romantic comedy, and then Max and I have a discussion afterward about respecting our partners and how communication is the key to any successful relationship."

Steve tossed popcorn at me.

"Hey!" I protested.

"You are such a liar. I bet you watch animated kids' movies every time."

I smirked, and he chucked another piece of popcorn at me, so I opened my mouth and leaned to the side, catching it with a satisfying crunch. "Thank you."

He opened a bag of chocolate-covered raisins and chucked one my way, but it bounced off my teeth. I scrambled after it. "Raisins are bad for dogs. So is chocolate." I grabbed it just before Obi did, his efforts to beat me hampered by the slippery hardwood floor.

"Sorry. You got it?" Steve asked, leaning forward to snag his collar and hold him back.

"Yep." I popped it in my mouth. "Did you have supper?"

"This is a bachelor supper." Steve dug his hand into the bag of popcorn. "How about this one?" He turned the screen of his tablet so I could see the title of a romantic comedy.

"You sure you're up for a discussion about the meaning of relationships and gender roles?" I teased.

"Maybe we could skip deciphering all that and just enjoy it. Or make out."

He laughed at my expression.

"I've wanted to see that one for a long time," I admitted, taking our escalating banter down a notch to let him know I appreciated his movie choice—one he'd no doubt never choose for himself.

"I hear there could be some scary parts, like a breakup," he said. "If you need to move over this way, I'll protect you."

"You're funny."

"Not cocky?"

"Not always. Just ninety-nine percent of the time."

My stomach rumbled again, and I mentally ran through my month's budget. We could order in, but December's heating bill was always one of the highest of the year, and I had already put quite a few Christmas gifts on my credit card despite trying to spread the cost out over the year.

Plus I'd just paid the unexpected cost of a post-secondary

application fee.

I really did need to change my life, didn't I?

"Pizza?" Steve asked.

"I'm on a budget." I put out a hand to stop him from speaking. "Don't say it."

"Say what?"

"That I should fight for more hours at the daycare, even though the other mom..." I shook my head. It didn't matter. In Steve's mind I was equally deserving, and nothing else mattered, because I was giving up something he felt was vitally important.

He scooted closer, well within arm's reach.

"Hey," he said softly. I faced him, ready for the lecture. "I like that you're kind, generous, and think of others. Those are good qualities, you know."

Blinking, I stared at him. The problem was being kind didn't always serve the best interests of myself or my family. It might even be construed as careless and irresponsible of me.

I felt ashamed for not standing up for myself and Max financially, and I made a vow that if the college accepted me, I would find a way to start taking those classes.

"And...?" I prompted Steve, certain there would be a jab coming after that compliment. We were long overdue for an argument, having spent several fight-free hours together.

He scooted a bit closer, his arm slung over the back of the cushions, near enough that I could feel the heat from his leg, his torso. He slowly brushed a thumb down my cheek. "Even though I don't always understand you, I think you're pretty special."

My heart warmed. Steve thought I was special. Even though I didn't live my life the way he felt I should. I wanted to freeze this moment. Frame it. Savor it.

"I would still like to kiss you," he stated, his thumb caressing my cheek, "though I'm pretty sure you'll say no."

❄

I STARED AT STEVE FOR A LONG MOMENT, THEN SUBTLY SHIFTED closer, my lips meeting his. He took the right amount of care, applied the right amount of pressure, and I sighed against him, folding myself into his arms to lengthen the kiss.

He was a good kisser.

"I think I like movie night," he murmured when we broke apart, my body still comfortably nestled in his embrace.

"I think I like being friends."

"Actually, I don't think that's a good idea."

"Why not?"

"Friends don't usually do this." He lifted my chin upward, giving me a sweet, short kiss.

"Hmm." He kissed me again. "That is problematic. I was intrigued by the idea of being your friend."

He tightened his grip, holding me close. He felt good. Strong. Capable.

I peered up at him. "You know that whatever we're doing together here, I'm not going to back down."

"Back down? About what?"

"Everything. Just because we kissed doesn't mean I'm not going to fight with you, or dish it back when you deserve it."

"I'm counting on it." He tucked me back against him before hitting the button to start the movie, his lips touching a kiss to my earlobe and sending shivers through me.

I didn't know whether to focus on the opening scenes or the fact that I'd kissed Steve. And liked it.

Was all that fighting between us really just chemistry, as Cassandra had suggested? I wasn't sure I was equipped to deal with a positive answer.

Which made me question what we were doing. I was a mom. I couldn't just float into a relationship or a fling or whatever this was with a man who was all about adventure and roaming the earth. Max would be home in less than a week and I needed to take care, have a plan, as well as minimize any impact my actions might have on my family.

And the last thing I had when it came to Steve was a plan.

My stomach rumbled and I sighed, allowing myself to fall deeper into his arms. I had soup in the fridge, but I'd have to get up to warm it for us, and might not get to snuggle in again if I left now.

Steve picked up his phone and, after a moment of him tapping and scrolling, I peeked at the screen. He was ordering pizza from the local craft brewery place. I'd heard it was the best in town, but had yet to try it.

"Would you like the house special?" he asked.

"Sounds amazing, but maybe we could scrounge something from the kitchen instead." I sat up, out of his arms. He was ordering an extra-large, and I already knew I wouldn't be able to reciprocate if there was a next time.

Next time.

Just live in the moment, Joy, because this likely won't happen again.

"I've got this," he said, his free arm bringing me back into his embrace. "I invited myself over. Remember?"

"You also rented the movie, as well as brought snacks and drinks."

"It's my duty to distract you, and I can't do that without pizza."

"You can't?" I asked doubtfully, as I watched him click the Order button. Pizza was on its way.

"Well, I could find ways, but I'm not sure you're game." His smile was wicked and I gave him a playful slap.

"I only do relationships," I said, trying to act prim and serious despite the flirty energy zipping through me. "I'm not a side adventure."

His expression became somber. "But you've given up rela-tionships."

I looked away. I had indeed said that.

"So we found a gray zone?" he asked.

I pulled my knees up to my chest, my heels hooked on the edge of the couch. "I don't know where we are." I needed to think, but my brain refused to help me out. All it could do was replay how good it felt to be in his arms.

Steve shifted, tugging my right foot so it could rest in his lap. He began kneading the ball, then glided his thumbs over the arch in the most delicious way. I let out a moan of contentment.

"Right there?" He glanced up as his thumb moved back to the spot that had made me moan.

I nodded, suddenly self-conscious. We were having a domestic moment.

Me and Steve.

And it felt natural. Good, even. As if the shutters of my life had been opened once again.

I should really create a plan, but a rebellious piece of me wanted to just savor having a man believe I was special, and to avoid considering any possible consequences.

"Gray zone, huh?" I mumbled, my muscles giving up their tightness as his thumbs worked their magic.

He watched me for a moment, then said, "We don't have to define our moments together. Max is away for a few days. We have time to explore without fear of hurting or confusing him."

My lips curved upward.

"I've always felt that gray is an underrated color." I was also starting to believe that Steve was pretty special, too.

IT WAS NEARLY MIDNIGHT WHEN STEVE SLIPPED BACK INTO HIS boots to trek through the dusting of snow that had fallen during our movie.

"Thank you for coming over. It was fun." I felt bashful, instinctively knowing that once Max was back this would end.

"You were a pretty good stand-in." I felt bad for the way I was distancing us, discounting the connection we'd had between kisses tonight.

Steve cast me a glance from the corner of his eye as he zipped up his coat.

I opened the door, flicking on the porch light. The timers had turned off my Christmas decorations hours ago, leaving Frosty deflated in the dark and making the night look like any other. Cold, slightly dreary and definitely lonely.

Calvin and Max hadn't called me tonight, having promised to do so tomorrow, since they'd been traveling most of today.

Calvin and I had agreed to spend Christmas Day together with Max, but I knew there would be a time when that would probably stop. Like, if one of us moved on. I opened my mouth to ask Steve why he didn't like Calvin, but realized it really didn't matter. Instead I said, "Feel free to invite yourself over anytime."

Behind me, Obi rolled over on his living room bed and let out a sigh so loud I could hear it from the doorway. He was waiting for me to call it a day so he could go off duty as my watchdog.

"I have to work tomorrow, but I'm sure you can think of a reason to get me to come over and help you cope tomorrow evening, too." Steve's smile was sly, knowing and slightly intoxicating. It made me want to roll up onto my toes, grab his face and kiss him.

I laughed. "I have no fun plans tomorrow night. Just work."

"At Little Comets?"

I shook my head. "A surprise for Max. I'm going to paint his room while he's away. So unless you want to help me, I suggest you pretend Jim has you working late, and then go catch a beer with the boys at the Tinsel and Tonic."

"Do you have everything you need? Paint? Brushes? Drop sheets?"

"You don't need to come slave away."

"Okay." He did that casual guy thing, with a shrug and a nod. He was considering something, but I wasn't sure what.

"Goodnight, Steve."

As I closed the door, I couldn't help wondering whether he would be coming over again tomorrow night, as well as why he hadn't given me a goodnight kiss.

CHAPTER 5

*a*fter spending the afternoon helping organize items for the community center's silent auction, I walked home, bundled up to my nose against a brisk wind. As I came in sight of Steve's empty driveway I was struck by a jab of disappointment.

Loneliness hit me hard. Empty house. No friendly smile next door. I sighed and continued up the sidewalk, letting myself in and Obi out. I unwrapped the layers of warm clothing, hanging everything up with determined care before letting the dog back in again.

Calvin and Max had video-chatted with me earlier, Max scowling and jet-lagged. But Calvin was optimistic about all that France could hold for the three of us, and I had simply nodded and smiled.

Maybe I wouldn't get accepted into the education program.

Maybe I would move to France and love it.

But if we were seriously considering Paris, why did I have a stash of painting materials currently sitting in my son's bedroom?

The paint was custom tinted, making it nonreturnable. Early that morning I'd filled boxes with stuffed animals, Lego and an impressive amount of Max's drawings, in preparation for painting.

Entering the room, I knelt down, pried open a can and considered the blue paint. Better than the beige for sure, but was it the right shade? It looked so... permanent and decisive. There would be nothing subtle about this change in color.

Obi clacked down the hallway, his nails suddenly quiet as he came onto the drop sheet-covered carpet beside me. He nudged me with his nose, then slid his wide, furry head under my arm.

"Hey, buddy." Our morning walk had been a bit shorter than usual, and guilt hit me. Just because I had wanted another twenty-five minutes of sleep, he'd paid the price with a quick jaunt, before I'd run out to buy paint and then headed off to help with the auction.

It would be dark in a few hours and I could paint all night. I couldn't walk him all night.

"Come on, let's go." I closed the can and leashed up Obi-Wan.

When we returned home a half hour later, Steve's truck was back in his driveway. I gave a goofy smile when I saw a note tacked to my door with duct tape.

With a bounce in my step I called out a cheery hello to my inflatable Frosty the Snowman before feeling silly and climbing the front steps to pull down the note.

I should get your phone number. The Chinese food I ordered is getting cold. If you're hungry you know where to find me.

I tried to fight my grin and lost.

Oh, I was hungry all right. Not just for the meal, but for the companionship, and having a man look at me like I might be something he'd want to consume.

My head popped up. Whoa. Where had that thought come from?

My cheeks heating, I reread the note. Steve still had that same scratchy, barely readable handwriting he'd had in high school. I'd been so certain that our group labs in chemistry would fail because of his illegible scrawl that I'd insisted on writing out every report myself.

For a moment I stood on my steps, undecided. I was playing with fire. People didn't change, and he'd been the thorn in my side all through school. If I went over to his place—like I wanted to—would I be getting into something I had no intention of pursuing?

If I didn't go over...

Empty house. Soup for supper. Painting a room blue. Alone.

Ugh.

I didn't like that option, either.

I wanted to spend time with Steve. To poke at him and be poked back. To laugh and kiss and carry on like I hadn't with a man in a very long time—since high school chemistry class, minus the kissing.

Plus I had to admit I was really curious about where this new friendship between Steve and me might go.

Unlocking the door, I unleashed Obi and set him free inside, fighting the doubts racing through my mind. Before I followed him in, a familiar voice called from next door, "Your furry Jedi master is welcome if he wants to come, too."

I leaned over the porch railing to get a better look at Steve's house. He had opened his screenless kitchen window and was hanging out to chat. It was so old-school I had to laugh.

I really needed to give that man my phone number.

"Okay," I hollered. "Can I bring anything?"

"Do you have any more gingerbread men?"

I shook my head.

Judith Smith was walking her dog and she paused, her steady, lopsided gaze moving from me to Steve and back again. With her voice loaded with what felt like a warning of some kind, she asked, "Has Calvin gone to France?"

"Yes, he has. He'll be back next week."

"Any kind of homemade cookies?" Steve called.

"I have some in the freezer. I can... donate some." I added the last part quickly, hoping Judith wouldn't get the wrong idea. The last thing I needed was something about Steve and me getting around town, when all that was happening was friendship.

"I didn't realize you were dating again," Judith said.

"I'm *not* dating." I heard the indignation in my voice, and then Steve's window slamming shut.

I told myself it was just an old window that needed force to be opened and closed, and that the slam wasn't indicative of how I'd inadvertently offended him. Because he should know that what we were playing at was never going to be real, so there was no reason to tell anyone about our confusing little gray zone. I was simply keeping him on his toes and he was keeping me from sinking into a lonely pit of despair. There was absolutely no need to make a royal mess of things by acting as though this was anything more than a temporary distraction for both of us.

STEVE'S HOUSE WAS DIFFERENT THAN I'D EXPECTED. INSTEAD OF mismatched furniture placed haphazardly throughout the rooms, the mismatched furniture was arranged in cozy, welcoming groups. Houseplants shared space with coasters and magazines on side tables. On the walls were photographs of glaciers, but instead of their blues and whites making the place feel cool, they somehow made it feel spacious and open.

"That's the Mendenhall Glacier up in Alaska," Steve said, as Obi trotted from room to room, lifting his nose to take in all that each space had to offer on an olfactory level.

"It's nice."

"I just about fell out of the helicopter taking that one." He pointed to another framed, blown-up photo.

"Are you serious?" I crossed my arms uncomfortably.

He grinned. "I was getting ready to ski, and I popped my

camera out from under my coat to take a quick shot just as the pilot pitched the helicopter to bank and land. I wasn't supposed to be leaning out like that."

"Always up for an adventure, aren't you?"

"I guess so." He gazed at the picture for a second longer.

"Do you sell your photos?"

He shook his head.

"What made you want to become a helicopter pilot?" I figured it was probably the rush of adrenaline. The ability to lift off and go where nobody else could. The imminent and constant pull of death or something.

"My dad used to fly. It always seemed..." He paused as though searching for words, and Obi nudged his hand, earning an absentminded ruffling of his ears.

"Romantic? Adventurous?"

"It's a shift in perspective. You lift above everything, and suddenly all that stuff weighing you down doesn't matter anymore. It's down there and you aren't."

I was silent for a moment, unsure what to say. What could possibly weigh down Mr. Freedom and Adventure?

"What do you run from?" I asked, my voice touched with uncertainty.

He gave me a funny look. "It's all still there when you land."

"Like what?" He was disrupting that entrenched view I had of him as someone with an easy-to-discard adventure addiction. Not some deep, wounded man with motivations that might possibly make my heart ache.

"The things you want but can't have."

We were staring at each other, and I was afraid to maintain the eye contact in case I began to read the subtext in his gaze, his words. This wasn't the Steve I knew, and I was afraid to confirm the hunch that was developing within me, blaring like a horn, disturbing my thoughts. It felt as though he was giving me a clue to something I wasn't sure I wanted to unearth, because knowing might mean change. Changing my thoughts and feelings.

I was the first to look away. "I heard you have food."

He hesitated for a second, then led me to the kitchen, which was clean and tidy, with everything in its place. Just like Calvin's kitchen. Although, granted, Calvin didn't have much in his house beyond the necessities and what he did had been chosen for its masculine appeal. I was currently in a *home*.

Steve got out plates and opened the boxes of Chinese takeout on the counter. I helped myself, not quite sure why I was over here eating his food when I had a bedroom to paint.

"Do you like Exploding Kittens?" he asked as he dished himself a heaping plate of food.

It was a card game that drove Max bonkers. Sometimes in a good way, sometimes not.

"Max adores it."

"Do you?"

I shrugged. "Max tends to get close to meltdown whenever he picks up the exploding kitten and doesn't have a defuse card." He was not yet familiar with the art of losing gracefully.

"Want to play?" Steve waved the box of cards as we sat at his kitchen table. My seat wobbled slightly, reassuring me in the oddest way.

"First one to explode loses," I said, taking the deck to sort and deal the cards. Obi trotted over and dropped at my feet, his eyebrows doing a dance as he watched first Steve, then me.

As we played, we ate, the food going down fast.

"Why did you want to become a doctor?" Steve asked partway through the game, his empty plate pushed to the side.

I shrugged, keeping my eyes on my cards as I reached down to ruffle the soft, long fur behind Obi's ears. It felt as though it was Steve's turn to disturb his view of me, and I wasn't sure I wanted him peeking into my soul like that. It felt as though he already understood me plenty.

"Afraid to tell me?" he asked casually. He'd picked up an exploding kitten and groaned. He had a defuse card, though, putting the kitten back into play and saving him from losing the game. But increasing my chances of a win.

"It was just something I wanted," I said, matching his easy tone. "You know how teens are."

"Teens want to help people?"

"Being able to heal someone is kind of a big thing," I said, feeling oddly defensive. "When else do you get to positively influence someone's life in such a way? You get to help return them to normal after something as potentially massive as life and death."

We played another few turns before he said, "You must've been devastated."

I folded my lower lip into my mouth. It still stung, letting go of that dream. It had been many years ago, but the loss and hurt hadn't waned as much as I'd have liked.

Maybe, I realized, because I hadn't filled the hole it had left.

"You know," I said, feeling miffed, "nobody seemed to even notice or care when I changed my dreams." I folded my cards facedown on the table. "I expected it to be this big deal, and everybody just kind of acted like... like nothing had happened. Like it was *better* that I wasn't going to med school."

My parents had been relieved. My mother had stated that it was good I wasn't going. She had worried that dealing with the stress of having people's lives in my hands on a daily basis might be too much, and that racking up massive student loans could break me financially.

"I cared," Steve said. He lowered his voice as he added, "I've seen women give up their dreams for men."

"It wasn't about Calvin!"

"Okay."

"Did you not see me almost faint out in my yard when Max had his nosebleed? Or catch me in biology class?"

He was fingering the cards in his hands, not looking up. "I think everybody gets wrapped up in their own world." He picked up a new card from the pile and revealed it. Another exploding kitten. "No defuse." He slid his hand of cards into the discard pile, having lost the game. "Sometimes people don't see what others are going through."

Like I hadn't seen the thing with his mom.

After gathering all the cards together, I reshuffled the deck, then set it aside. "You know why I didn't become a doctor. Why did you act like I'd given up? You all but implied that I was latching on to Calvin—who never truly loved me, by the way—so I wouldn't have to deal with my own inadequacies. That I gave up out of fear. That I'm complaisant, or too unambitious, and that it's to my own detriment. That when things get difficult I roll over."

My voice had grown loud and I suddenly felt Obi's nose against my thigh. I realized I was standing, hands clenched into fists.

"Do you?" Steve asked, his tone careful and quiet.

"No!" I was disgusted that this man who seemed to know so much about me was doubting me. Doubting my strength and ability to take control of my own life. "I tried, okay? I tried self-hypnosis. I borrowed audiobooks from the library to listen to every night. I did everything I could think of to try and get over the issue. I even had this whole mantra about how everything was okay even if somebody was bleeding. None of it worked. I *tried.*"

Steve reached forward and touched my hand, the gesture warm and unexpected.

I yanked it back. "Giving up those scholarships was the hardest thing I ever had to do. And I hate that you think I hit a roadblock and gave up without even trying."

It hurt more than everyone just going along with my drastic switch in life plans.

Steve shook his head, not saying anything. Finally he murmured, "It's none of my business."

"What isn't?" I snapped. "You're an open book, remember?"

"Is that why you focused on marrying Calvin?" He was looking at me, his eyes full of questions and hurt. "Even though maybe marriage wasn't quite as much as you needed?"

I swallowed hard and stared at him, but he didn't apologize, change the subject or take the question back, like my ex-husband would have. I took my plate and put it in the dishwasher, giving myself a moment to cool down.

"You're the only one who ever challenged me about swapping med school for a wedding band," I said. "You know that?"

"Maybe it's because I cared more than anyone else."

I let out a bitter laugh. "Yeah, right."

"Maybe I *saw* how much you wanted to become a pediatrician. Maybe because I've seen women give up their careers, their dreams, for men who love them. Love isn't enough to fill the hole, and I've seen it kill them. Is it wrong that maybe I wanted more for you?"

There was a fire in his eyes that was familiar, yet new. Like the flame that had licked behind every fight we'd ever had, but different today. Big enough to consume both of us if let out of control.

I'd never had anyone fight me the way he was. I didn't know how to respond, what to say. All I could do was feel awash in that same old hurt and disappointment that had haunted me since I was a teen.

"And maybe I just wanted you to be happy for me—because it was my choice." I was almost at the front door when I heard him speak from his spot in the kitchen.

"But maybe I could see that you weren't entirely happy with it."

"Maybe my happiness *is* none of your business," I muttered under my breath, shoving my arms into my coat sleeves.

"My dad traveled with the military as a helicopter pilot," Steve said, his voice carrying. I paused, unsure whether I could truly walk out in a huff when his tone told me he was about to reveal something. "My mom used to be the chief financial officer for Cohen's Blissful Body Care in South Carolina—somehow managing her career despite how we moved around from base to base. She loved it. She was made for it. But she gave it up for my dad. For me."

I stepped back to the kitchen doorway.

"She wasn't happy at home, and she got sick. She became a shell..." He paused and swallowed, but then his voice filled with conviction as he met my eye. "You *have* to fulfill your dreams. You *have* to pursue life. You can't waste it."

I nodded to let him know I'd heard him.

"Let absolutely nobody stand in the way of what you want. Nobody."

THE KITCHEN FELT SMALL, ELECTRIFIED, AS THOUGH IF EITHER ONE of us took a step we'd bring the walls down.

I stood in the doorway, frozen to the spot. As a teen, every once in a while Steve would get like this. He'd tighten up, clam up, then skip chemistry class. But there was no class to skip tonight, just me.

He suddenly pushed his chair back and marched over to where I stood. His eyes a churning sea of emotion, he scooped his hands into my hair, tangling his fingers in the strands, bracing my entire being with his for one long glorious moment before locking his lips on mine in a fervent kiss. He took my breath away with the intensity and ferocity of his need. I kissed him back, lost in the feeling of being consumed by him.

Panting, we broke apart.

"Wow," I breathed.

He pulled me in for another long kiss, this one slower.

"I couldn't become a doctor," I said, when it finally ended.

"I know."

Somehow he had seen what I had refused to. He'd seen that Calvin couldn't fill that big, empty hole that my lost dream had made. That was why he had been against me getting married after high school.

But this time I could see things just fine.

"This isn't going to work," I whispered.

He kissed me again, that urgent need rising between us once more. It made me light-headed while at the same time grounding me. I felt lost, but found. It was as though two contradictory universes were spinning through me, and I was powerless to do anything but turn with them.

"Never sell yourself short," he said between kisses.

"Take your own advice," I retorted, kissing him back.

He pulled away to look at me. "What does that mean?"

"You put up walls. You run to a new adventure instead of staying through the quiet. You fight instead of bonding."

"We're not fighting."

And we were bonding. Did that make me a liar?

His kisses turned tender, his hands secure on my back, my waist. "What if you met someone who could love you the way you needed? What would you do?"

I was unsure of the territory he was leading us into. "What are you saying?"

"I think you could be a lot happier, Joy Evans."

He gently tipped my chin upward so I'd be forced to look at him. And maybe so I'd consider him. The idea scared me.

"I'm happy enough."

"You have everything you want in your life?" His eyes were on my lips as he brushed the hair from my face.

"I applied to go back to school."

I shouldn't have told him that.

I knew he wouldn't let me reverse my decision about going if I got accepted, but it also meant he would hold me to a lot of other things, too. It would be good for me—as long as I didn't break from the pressure.

His spine straightened. "Good. Don't give up on what *you* want. Don't put the needs of others…"

"Your mom's history is not repeating itself through me, Steve."

He dropped his arms, his face suddenly expressionless.

"Seriously, Steve. Let me live my life my way. They're my mistakes to make."

He took a step back.

I didn't know how to navigate this. His reaction suggested I'd hurt his feelings or crossed a line. But this was us—we fought and threw daggers, without injury. At the moment, though, it felt as if we were unearthing things that could cause wounds in both of us. We were in landmine territory, and I didn't know how to avoid them. One moment it felt as though he was throwing bombs at my feet, shrapnel and dirt flying up at me. The next moment he was pulling me out of harm's way.

"Don't put others first, Joy." His tone was quiet.

"You do understand how disruptive going back to school would be?"

"Tell me about France."

France. The air left my lungs. France was a problem. One I didn't want to talk about with Steve.

"It's beautiful." I had crossed my arms and now lowered them to my sides, but found them landing on my hips instead. "There are job opportunities for engineers. The people over there speak French, and their food is supposed to be divine."

"Tell me about how *you* feel about France."

"I don't want to move there," I blurted out. I whirled away from him, curse words running through my mind. I had not meant to say that.

"Then don't."

"Yeah? And how's that going to work?" Tears filled my eyes as I faced him again. "I'm a mom. I don't get to be self-centered, Steve. And maybe your mom didn't either. Being part of a family means being well-acquainted with give-and-take. Maybe she stayed home because she loved you, and being your mother was what mattered most to her. Maybe her getting sick was unrelated."

I turned away once again, blindly making my way toward the door.

As I fumbled into my winter boots, Steve stood close enough to touch. I looked up at him with an ache in my chest. I feared speaking, because it would surely unlatch the gate holding back the tears I was fighting.

"If something isn't working for one of the family members," he said, "chances are it won't be working for everyone else before long."

I shakily zipped up my coat, but before I could march out the door, Steve swept me into a hug, enclosing me in his warmth, his heart pounding under my ear. "Don't be like me. Don't run away."

"I thought you wanted me to be like you," I said in a choked voice, "and have the world bend around me."

He didn't answer, just kissed me with a tenderness that confused me even further.

CHAPTER 6

"I'm coming, I'm coming," I grumbled, shuffling toward the front door. I rubbed the sleep from my eyes and smoothed my hair. The knocking had stopped and Obi had ceased barking after only two bellows, which meant the person was either gone or was someone he knew.

I'd had a late night painting Max's room and going over all I'd said to Steve before that. Of course I wanted to go to France. I wanted to be with my family. Was I losing my mind, saying what I had to him? Now he'd never let it go, and he would pester me mercilessly if I didn't pull the plug on leaving town, should the tentative plan ever come to fruition.

But why was Steve, if he was so into adventures, encouraging me to stay home? Why wasn't he telling me to go?

I opened the door to find myself face-to-face with him. Steve was smiling, and looked perky and well rested.

"You again?" I asked, as Obi—the big traitor—leaned against Steve's long legs, his big doggy eyes adoring as he waited for some love.

"You're cute when you're all groggy." Steve had an affectionate warmth in his gaze as he handed me an insulated cup of coffee.

Didn't he understand fighting? You didn't just come over the next morning as if everything was good again.

I hoisted the cup like I was toasting him, and went to swing the door shut. There hadn't been nearly enough hours between our tough words and this morning for me to feel fully sorted out. Not to mention our kisses.

He stopped the door from closing. "I have a surprise. Put on some clothes."

Didn't he feel the need to rehash last night's fight? Prove to me that I'd been in the wrong?

When I refused to budge Steve tipped his head to the side, watching me for a moment. "I'm sorry if I was bossy last night."

"I'm fine with moving to France." My words seemed to have no impact. "And I'm happy," I added.

"Okay."

"And I won't take back my words. About... any of it." Even if I may have stepped over the line.

He didn't look quite as perky, but gave me a nod. "Fine."

I waited for him to defend his side of the argument. He didn't. "So?"

I didn't know where to go from here. I'd created some mighty big plans on how I could avoid him for the next few days, weeks, maybe even months.

"We're good?" he asked.

"No, we're not good." Moving past fights wasn't supposed to be this easy. Where was the guilt trip for how I'd treated him, for the words I'd slung? Wasn't he going to act wounded and draw out his hurt forever? It felt like I was getting off easy for speaking my mind so freely. "Don't meddle."

"Hmm." He looked down at his feet with a frown.

"Okay! So I could handle making some changes in my life. You're right! School will be good. If I get in, I'm going. Even though it's going to cause a major mess." I watched him carefully.

There was no gloating? No grin of victory? "So be happy you were right, and win this one."

He was still staring at his feet as if he had something to hide.

"What did you do?" I asked.

He looked up, appearing contrite. "To be fair, I didn't know about the no-meddle rule."

I waved the coffee cup he'd given me. "You're not going to let me go enjoy this in peace, are you?"

He shook his head and took a step closer, so I'd back into the house. "Go put some clothes on."

I sighed in defeat. "Fine. Give me a minute. I have to walk Obi-Wan anyway. We are walking, right?"

He nodded and I hurried to my bedroom, where I yanked on a pair of faded jeans and a sweatshirt, before running to the bathroom to splash water on my face and wrangle my hair into a ponytail. Moments later I was standing beside Steve along with my dog.

"Where are we going?"

"Not far."

I had a feeling I might know where Steve was taking me, and I was buzzing with anticipation to find out if I was correct.

AS WE CLIMBED THE CREAKING STEPS TO THE COMMUNITY CENTER, I knew that whatever Steve's surprise was had to do with the piano.

"Calvin promised to deal with the piano," I said, carefully avoiding the spot on the steps where ice had formed. Steve didn't need to know that Calvin had given up already.

He unlocked the door. Obi stood with his nose in the crack, ready to go in first. I unclipped his leash so he wouldn't drag me into the doorjamb.

Steve moved inside, feeling his way down the wall, on a

search for the light switches to brighten the room. Onstage, Obi ran his nose along the length of the piano bench before giving a huff and moving on with his tour of inspection. The piano was off-center, not quite under one of the bright stage lights.

Steve and I climbed the stairs to the stage and he flipped up the keys' cover, then gestured for me to sit. "I was watching some YouTube videos last night."

Ha! So he hadn't had a perfect night's rest, either. Somehow that made me feel better.

"I still don't have all the tools or pieces I need, but see if this is better."

I hesitated, then slowly eased onto the bench. "You tuned the piano?" And had done some legwork to track down the center's key as well.

"You be the judge of that."

I poised my fingers over the keys, not sure what to expect other than disappointment. I inhaled, then let out the breath as I began, playing a song I'd soon be performing with my friends on Christmas Day.

When I'd finished, I ran my fingers up the keys once again, noting that the dead one was still silent.

"I ordered a new key. Glue didn't work," Steve said. "Did you know that they have piano graveyards, kind of like a wrecker for cars? You can order used parts."

"No, I didn't," I said. The piano sounded surprisingly better. Was that because I was expecting it to be awful, or had he actually improved it?

"What do you think?" he asked, when I continued to play. He was leaning against the side of the piano, his arms crossed over the top.

"It's definitely better." I paused my playing and tapped the silent key thoughtfully, then glanced up at him, startled by his intense gaze. "Do you think the key will arrive in time?"

He shrugged. "Nobody will notice if you miss a note or play

an octave or two higher or lower than usual."

Other than killing my poor friends as they tried to match the pitch. Still, I had to give Steve points for trying.

"Don't pour too much money into it." I sucked on the insides of my cheeks, mulling over the piano issue. Steve's fix might pass for one night.

"Can you sing?" Steve asked, nudging me aside with his hip as he settled on the bench beside me.

"What?"

He began to play a song that sounded disjointed and out of tune. In other words, perfectly Steve and in sync with the old piano.

"What are you playing?" I leaned closer, intrigued.

"You don't know it?"

I shook my head. The tune picked up tempo and I marveled at Steve's hidden talent. It reminded me of discovering a well-hidden chocolate egg a week after Easter—after you'd already eaten your stash and were craving another hit of chocolate.

He began singing, his voice low and gravelly. The kind of voice that would fit someone found eating a can of beans under a bridge, ready to scare you witless.

I knew this song.

"Tom Waits?" I breathed, as his fingers danced faster and faster. "Nobody knows Tom Waits."

Steve kept playing. "A girl in high school got me hooked."

I frowned at him. I was quite certain nobody else in Christmas Mountain High had been listening to this artist.

"I snuck a listen on her iPod when she went to the bathroom during chem," he explained.

"I knew I couldn't trust you," I murmured, starting to sway with Steve as he continued to play "Just the Right Bullets." I was about ready to dive in as well, until he got to the second-to-last verse. The lyrics. The singer wanted the subject of the song to be happy. It was his only wish, and that he'd fix things for her—fix everything to make her happy.

I couldn't help but feel as though Steve had chosen this song on purpose, and that it was saying more than I was willing to hear. I slid off the end of the bench, a lump in my throat.

"Nobody knows Tom Waits," I repeated in a whisper, hugging myself on the chilly stage, the empty room echoing the song back at us.

Steve stopped playing, then smoothed dust off the keys, making them shine. Neat and tidy. Black and white. Almost perfect.

"I do," he replied just as quietly.

But why?

"It's still out of tune."

"But getting closer?"

I couldn't meet his eye. Couldn't quite consider the subtext, the deeper meaning behind his words.

"It has a ways to go before it'll be what I need."

WE WALKED BACK TO THE HOUSE TOGETHER, MY STOMACH rumbling due to missing breakfast, Obi tugging on his leash to sniff at every tree we passed.

"Come heli-skiing with me this afternoon," Steve said, when we were about a block from home. "There's this gorgeous slope you've got to ski to believe."

Jumping out of a helicopter to ski down an ungroomed and possibly unstable terrain just for the rush of it didn't appeal to me.

Maybe eight or so years ago, when I was still instructing at the Blacktail Mountain Ski Area and loving every second of ripping down the slopes on skis. Now, not so much. I was a bit more careful with anything potentially dangerous, giving risky sports a wide berth, well aware of their power to upset my life.

"I don't ski anymore." And I certainly wasn't going to jump out of a helicopter to refresh that skill.

"Why not?"

"I'm a mom."

"You're not teaching Max how to ski? I thought parents were all about getting their kids into outdoor sports so they'd spend more time being physically active."

"You're not supposed to instruct your family or friends. It's part of being certified."

"So?"

"So?" Rules were in place for a reason—to protect people.

Great. Now I wanted to take Max out to see if he might love the sport as much as I had.

"Then come fly with me this afternoon. A quick helicopter ride is less risky than driving most days."

"Most days?" I repeated doubtfully.

He didn't reply, just watched me debate playing hooky with putting the second coat of paint on Max's bedroom walls.

"Let's go play," Steve urged. "Let me show you the town from above."

"You think I need to run away from my problems?"

"They'll all still be there when you land."

"You think I need perspective then?"

"Why can't you let loose and play with me?"

"Why do you always push?"

He was standing close, as though he wanted to touch me. "Because I want to see you smile."

I gave him a grotesque grin. "Satisfied?"

"Nope. It's not the same as your loving-life smile."

I couldn't even recall what that smile felt like anymore.

Before I could indulge in a mini pity party, he said, "I'll pick you up in half an hour."

"With your helicopter? Funny."

"Are you scared?"

I paused to think about it. Not exactly scared. But I wasn't eager.

But why shouldn't I take him up on his offer of a free helicopter ride? Why leave all the fun for the tourists? Hadn't I promised myself I would do something exciting for myself during this break?

No, I hadn't.

Why hadn't I? Didn't I deserve it? And wouldn't it be exciting to have some of my own news to share when Max and Calvin called?

I should do more than just watch movies rated higher than PG-13, stay up past my regular bedtime, and paint a bedroom.

"Yes." I gave a firm nod, as though assuring myself of my decision.

"You're scared?" Steve touched my elbow and said seriously, "Because as a pilot, I've never had a crash I couldn't walk away from."

"Funny. I'm actually taking you up on that helicopter ride. But you have to pack our lunch, and I'm not paying for fuel."

He looked affronted. "It wouldn't be a very good date if I asked you to do that."

Before I could protest that this was *not* a date, Steve skipped over the snowy banks, cutting across his yard. He jogged up the steps and turned to me with a wide grin before letting himself in the house.

There were no two ways about it. That man was determined to secure a place in my inner circle whether I held the door open for him or he had to break it down himself.

"It's not a date," I said to Steve, as the helicopter lifted off. I'd had almost an hour to work through the shock of him wrangling me into something outside my comfort zone, as well as implying it was a date. Was I so out of the loop that I didn't understand what dating was like beyond high school?

"You have to turn on your microphone," he told me, flicking a lever so we could talk through our bulky headsets.

I kept my mouth shut.

"What was it you said?" he asked as we rose into the air, the big machine tipping to combat a gust of wind, the world around us a swirling cloud of snow.

I clung to my seat. What was I doing? I was a mom. I had a child.

I ventured a look through the side window, to find the ground racing away as we climbed higher. My hands clenched into fists and I reminded myself to breathe.

Then we were zipping along the valley, not so close to the ground that I worried about hitting trees or disturbing wildlife, but still not high enough that I felt entirely safe.

I ordered myself to relax.

"You'd better not crash," I said.

"Don't worry, I got my license to fly out of a cereal box." He winked at me in a way that made my stomach give a little flip and my cheeks warm. Despite our past and our fights I liked this guy. Putting the physical risk of a helicopter ride aside, I reminded myself that good moms didn't date casually, and with Steve it would never be anything but.

As we flew past a meadow, I saw a herd of elk pawing at the snow to graze on the dried grasses beneath. We moved higher.

"Where are we going?" I asked.

"Do you always stress out this much when someone else is driving?"

I stayed quiet, thinking for some reason of the book about the divorcée Carol had given me. Its message was learning not to care so much about the perception others had of us, but daring to believe something new about ourselves.

Currently, it seemed everyone was nudging me about how I was living my life a bit too safely, and as a result, putting myself at risk by being too sheltered. An obvious example was how I relied on Calvin, to the detriment of my long-term financial health.

I leaned back against the seat, eyes closed, concentrating.

So if my friends were right, the next question might be who was I, and was I the person I wanted to be? Obviously, I felt I could be more as I'd applied for school. But beyond that, my mind went blank, refusing to answer anything further. I slowly opened my eyes, to discover we were already near the top of the tall mountains, thousands of feet above sea level. Steve was watching me with concern, probably regretting taking me out, and worried that I was in the middle of a quiet meltdown. Maybe I was. Melting down my old self-image.

We rose above the puffy clouds that had been lying low over the town, and were suddenly blinded by sunshine. It was breathtaking, nothing but clouds, trees and snowy mountaintops. And us.

"Wow."

"There's a little bowl where the receding glacier left a lake over here. I've heard that in the summer it's stunning. Crystalline blue waters like you've never seen." He banked the helicopter to head in the direction he'd tipped his head, causing me to squeal. It didn't feel dangerous, just different. It shook things loose in my box of internal worries.

We flew for several more minutes, Steve pointing out various mountains like a guide, even taking me past a slope covered with ski tracks where he had dropped someone off to go heli-skiing yesterday.

I wondered if he had taken this job to give him daily perspective. I understood if he did.

When he finished his tour of the local valley, he turned the chopper to head back toward home. As we drew near the town, I could feel the weight of my life pressing back in. All my so-called problems were still waiting for me, just like he'd promised.

"Aren't we having lunch?" For some reason I'd expected Steve to put the helicopter down near a secluded cabin, somewhere we could have a hot lunch.

Ridiculous.

I'd obviously been watching far too many movies, and hadn't had nearly enough dates in my lifetime.

"Trust me, Joy. I keep my promises."

"A picnic then?" It was winter, but not completely unheard of... What if his idea of lunch was going to Prancer's Pancake House? The whole town would have their tongues flapping if we showed up there together, and I knew I'd have a negative knee-jerk reaction about my attraction to Steve if they did. I needed more time to accept my change of heart so I didn't automatically and publicly reject him.

He pointed into the valley near Christmas Mountain. "Looks like Ashley has a sleigh ride going on."

"I've barely seen her since coming home. She's been so busy with her new business." I looked down, sorting out where we were and where the ride was taking place. "Actually, that might be Faith Sterling! I can't believe there's talk about closing down the luxury tour company. I hope she teaches that city snob Adam how important that business is, and shows him how wonderful and healthy it is to get out in nature."

Steve made a hum of agreement. A moment later he asked, "Have I convinced you how awesome helicopter rides are?" He gave me a quick glance as he maneuvered the chopper down to the helipad just outside of town.

"It was nice," I said, downplaying how thrilling it had been, before catching myself. "Actually, it was really great. Thank you."

"You're welcome."

When he'd successfully touched down, he stated, "Another landing where everyone can walk away."

"Don't worry about adding lunch to our date. This was enough."

"I thought you said this wasn't a date."

"And I thought you said you couldn't hear me without the microphone thingy turned on?"

He smirked and turned off the helicopter's engine.

"Thank you, Steve."

"You're welcome."

We smiled at each other for a moment, and I was unable to hide my growing grin. "I feel like the kids at the daycare when I told them Santa is coming to visit tomorrow."

"Yeah?"

"Miles Wilson is dressing up in a suit."

"Mr. Wilson? Who owns the feed store? You're joking!"

I smiled. The man was a natural Santa with his wild white hair and wonderful green eyes. Yes, he was commonly known as the biggest grump in town, but he was a softie on the inside and I knew the kids would adore him.

"Well, that's fun. I'm sure they'll get a kick out of their lumps of coal," Steve muttered, and I laughed at his lack of faith.

"I love this time of year." Even people like Mr. Wilson got into the spirit of the season.

Steve removed his headset and opened his door. I continued to sit in the seat for a second, thinking.

"Are you coming?" he asked.

"Where?"

"Stop asking questions and just go with the flow."

"Maybe I'm used to controlling things so I don't have children melt down on me."

"I don't see any here today."

I climbed out of the helicopter and met Steve on the other side. "I'm not used to going with the flow."

"Do you trust me?" he asked.

I could trust him to scramble my mind, create havoc with my emotions and to do the unexpected. I could trust him to help Max. I could trust him to be kind to my dog. And I'd just climbed into a helicopter and allowed him to fly me to the skies, opening my world to a whole new perspective.

Steve was a man who came from a good place, even though he made me want to pull my hair out half the time.

"Maybe I shouldn't have asked that," he said, working his way through a system of securing the helicopter before taking a half step back to survey his work, then turning in the direction of his truck.

"And maybe you need to learn patience." I caught up with him, hooking my right hand in the crook of his elbow as I matched his pace.

"Patience hasn't served me well in the past." There was something going on, moving behind his eyes, darkening them.

"When you're patient people can fully consider their reply. It may give them enough time to realize how deeply they do trust you, for example. But if you would rather race off to the next thing..." I let go of his arm and he stopped walking. "I guess it's no big deal, Adventureman."

He frowned at the name and I realized that somehow Steve Jorgensen—despite all our differences—had woven his way into my inner circle. And while I didn't know what I was going to do about it, I vowed to explore it, and that meant living a little bit more in the present moment. Starting now.

I rolled up onto my tiptoes on the edge of the frozen helipad and kissed Steve full on the lips.

Steve pulled over at the Overlook, up the hill from Christmas Mountain. Down below, chimneys on what looked like tiny toy houses were puffing out warm air, creating clouds above them as their furnaces ran.

"Come on," he said, climbing out of his truck.

If I recalled correctly, this was where Morgan and Dallas had gotten engaged last Christmas. I didn't have any ridiculous thoughts about Steve proposing to me, but I stayed in the truck just the same.

He gave me a questioning look as I glanced out the windshield, checking our surroundings, then asked through his open door, "Do you have to know everything about everything at every moment of every day?"

"How many times can you say 'every'?" I quipped.

"Many, many times." He opened the back door to his pickup and pulled out a backpack and a blanket that I had assumed were part of a winter emergency kit.

Steve walked down a short, packed path to the bench that overlooked the town. He draped the blanket over it to protect us from the icy seat, then opened the backpack and started pulling out food.

"Picnic," I said to myself, finally climbing from the truck. He was indeed a man of his word.

I sat beside him on the bench.

A helicopter ride, a kiss and a picnic.

It was a date.

"Hungry?" Steve handed me a container holding several kinds of sliced cheese. He opened a box of crackers, then a small tub with grapes and strawberries—two of the more pricey fruits found in the Christmas Mountain grocery store at this time of year. Definitely date food.

Next he pulled out a bottle of what looked like champagne, and I found myself glancing over my shoulder for Officer Hutchinson. The policewoman was still considered new to town, despite having been here for more than a year. She was a bit of a stickler for rules, and had nailed Ashley with a speeding ticket last year when she'd coasted into town above the posted limit. I had a feeling Ms. Hutchinson would not appreciate us drinking on public land.

"Relax," Steve said, catching my expression. "It's just sparkling grape juice."

"Isn't that a roundabout way of saying champagne?"

He let out a laugh and unfurled the foil from around the cork. "It's non-alcoholic."

I picked up one of the plastic cups. "Well, if it won't send me to jail, then it's not worth it." I made a show of pulling my glass away.

"You enjoyed your one and only night in the clink?"

The pig incident.

"I wasn't in there all night." I hesitated, then added, "I saw you across the street when I got released."

"Yep. I saw you, too."

"You were smirking."

"Because the perfect Joy Evans had done something that surprised me."

"That's not why."

"And because..." He was smiling up at the trees and I had a feeling it was at my expense.

"Releasing farm animals into a school is not funny," I said, quoting my mother.

"But it was, wasn't it?" He snagged my glass, filling it for me.

I thought of my friends and how they'd come alive, laughing and giggling. Even the straight-laced Lexi Townshead had gotten into the prank. "It was kind of fun."

"Want to go paint our names on the water tower?" Steve asked, tilting his head toward the town's main reservoir.

"No," I said definitively.

"Remember that guy from Blueberry Springs who fell off their tower back in high school? What was his name again?"

"Frankie Smith. He was trying to impress my cousin Mandy.

Did you hear she painted his name up there and got busted like he did? She didn't fall off, though."

I took a sip of the sparkling juice. It was pretty good and its bubbles made the picnic feel special—like this was a celebratory moment. Our first date. I set my cup down beside me to hide the tremors that had started in my hand.

"Why were you really smirking?" I asked, realizing he hadn't fully answered my earlier question.

He shrugged, shoving a cracker in his mouth.

"You can't get out of answering by stuffing your face."

He chewed, then replied confidingly, "I wasn't actually smirking. I thought maybe you were rebelling. You know, about to change up your life. I was curious."

"Change it how?"

"It doesn't matter."

"Tell me."

His gaze got a faraway look like he was lost in his thoughts, and I wondered if teenaged Steve had thought I was about to dump Calvin and find a way to become a doctor.

Steve's focus returned, and he said cheerily, "I was going to bail you out if your parents didn't."

I shifted toward him, taken off guard—although not surprised —by him choosing to change the subject. But I didn't know what to say. Bail was not exactly a teenager's part-time-work kind of money. Not that my parents had needed to post it. Instead I'd gotten a lecture from every adult I knew, and us girls had spent the next morning cleaning the school hallways where the pigs had run, and doing our best to fix the football trophy case. But still, to think that Steve was there to make sure I was okay touched me deeply.

I had spent every minute inside that jail cell thinking my parents weren't going to come, that they'd be too humiliated to claim me. And that they would let me sit so I could learn a lesson

I already knew: the one time I had chosen to go with the flow and be a bit mischievous had landed me in jail.

"Thank you," I said to Steve.

"I didn't do anything."

"But you were there." I locked my cold hand over his, giving it a squeeze.

"I'm glad they came," he said, taking a sip of his drink with his other hand.

"Why?"

"It would have been pretty awkward if you hadn't accepted my help."

"True." And I likely wouldn't have. My pride and self-assurance that he was evil and always plotting against me with judgment in his heart would have surely had me soundly rejecting any offer.

But now? Now he was warming my heart in the most unexpected ways.

CHAPTER 7

*C*hristmas was right around the corner and the kids in the daycare were pretty much bonkers. I loved every second of it, even though they had been bouncing off the walls and asking me every five minutes when Santa was coming.

Originally, Miles Wilson was supposed to pop by just after lunch, but his wife had called earlier to say he was down for the count with the stomach flu. Our last-minute quest to find someone to wear the suit had failed, and just after lunch I'd broken the news that Santa couldn't make it to the daycare. They'd taken it like troopers. Troopers who'd lost their platoon in a horrifying and grueling war.

I'd been about five seconds from putting on the suit myself.

Kneeling on the floor, I took three-year-old Anya Rogers's hands in mine and gently curled down a few fingers. "This many sleeps until Santa comes to your house."

She wiggled and grinned at me.

"Do you think you can wait that long?" I asked.

Anya shook her head.

"Maybe we could make some reindeer food. Have you done that before?"

She shook her head again.

"That settles it. Let's get the rest of the kids and make some reindeer food for Rudolph and his friends."

Like the little leader she was, Anya gathered up the few classmates whose families weren't yet on holiday, and we settled at one of the low tables to get started. We had only ten kids, which was fine for Edith and me to care for—when she wasn't busy in her office.

"Do you know what helps reindeer fly?" I asked. No Santa Claus visit meant we were gliding right on into our regularly scheduled craft time.

"Snowshoes!" replied Elias, who then burst into giggles.

"Ice cream," another said.

"Wings?" asked Anya.

I held up a tiny container of glitter. "This does." I held up a small bag. "And they love oats. So what we do is we mix these two things together, and then on Christmas Eve sprinkle it out on the snow where you think Santa might land his sleigh, so the reindeer can eat it."

"I'm not allowed on the roof," said Evan.

"Sometimes they land in our yards," I said, "and I bet if you put some in the front yard they'll eat it. They aren't always hungry, though. If they don't eat it, the birds will."

"Is glitter safe for birds?" asked my boss as she glided by. Edith was like a harbinger of gloom, the way she coasted silently over the floor, popping up to make me doubt the wisdom of anything I did. I looked at the glitter. Surely birds would avoid eating it, wouldn't they?

But now I wasn't so sure.

I had a momentary vision of the kids climbing on their roofs, and birds becoming ill from eating glitter.

"It's fine," I said, reading the label. The glitter was edible, Edith just causing me to doubt myself. It seemed to be a favored pastime of hers.

The kids and I set to work, and by the time we were done I was yawning. I'd been so excited from my so-called date with Steve last night that I'd stayed up late, putting the second coat of paint on Max's room, and more than once imagining what it might be like to date Steve Jorgensen for real.

"Okay, put your reindeer food in your cubby," I told the kids, "then find a stuffy to snuggle with. It's story time!"

Story time. Then nap time. Everything was right on schedule —the only way to keep a roomful of tykes from extreme meltdown.

The little ones circled around me on the carpet as I opened our afternoon story about a snowman. The front door of the daycare opened, kicking the furnace into gear as it battled the draft of winter air. It was Anya's mom, Emily Rogers, the principal of the elementary school. "Guess who I found outside?" she announced loudly.

I did a quick head count. None of the children were missing. Before I could ask whom she'd found, a man came in dressed in a red-and-white suit.

Santa.

The kids went wild, storming the baby gate that separated them from the front entry, where Santa stood with Emily. The kids shouted, "Santa! Santa! He came! You told a lie, Miss Joy. He's here! He's here!"

"I'm so glad he could make it."

I glanced up as Santa's head raised, and familiar blue eyes greeted me with warmth as my breath caught in my chest.

STEVE.

Steve was saving the day by dressing up as Santa. Any lingering uncertainty about him dissolved, and I swear my ovaries twitched as I battled the urge to swoon. Just a little.

Just... you know. Having a man you kind of like dress up as Santa to save the day was a noteworthy item on the mental does-he-check-out list.

Steve let out a booming "Ho, ho, ho!" and the kids' excitement level ratcheted up another notch.

"I saw Steve outside C.M. Salon after getting my hair done by Morgan," Emily whispered in my ear. "And when he heard you didn't have a Santa he offered to step in." She beamed at Steve in a way that made jealousy rise inside me. She was *married*.

Then again, ovaries were ovaries and I was certain hers were twitching, too.

"Who is this?" Santa asked. "Joy Evans? My, you're all grown up. Do you have a boyfriend?" He was watching me with dancing eyes, and I felt the heat rise in my face as the kids giggled.

I might have to mentally uncheck a box or two on the does-he-check-out list if he continued on.

"Miss Joy! Kiss Santa!" Anya called, starting another round of giggles.

Emily opened the baby gate for Steve and he closed in on me, asking, "Have you been a good girl?" He wasn't even five minutes inside the daycare and he was already knocking everything off-kilter.

"Okay, boys and girls, go to the carpet so we can let Santa come in and join us."

I began directing the children toward the sitting area, but Steve stopped me. He was digging in his bag. "Do you boys and girls want to know what I have?"

They all raced back to him.

He had palmed a box roughly the size of a basketball and was holding it over his head. "This present says it's for Miss Joy."

My head snapped to Steve. He'd brought me a gift? When had he had time to pull that off? Unless this was something slipped into the bag by Edith, when she'd set it up for Miles. I considered the idea and quickly discarded it. This was one hundred percent Steve.

"Me! Me! I want one, too!" Anya was bouncing in front of Steve, yanking at his sleeve as he approached me.

"She's been extra good and is often forgotten." He nudged me, handing over the gift. "Go ahead. Open it."

I didn't know what to expect. Something over-the-top? Ridiculous? Embarrassing? Telling?

"I'll open it in a bit." The box was a tad heavier than I'd expected, and I tucked it in the crook of my arm. "Let's get the kids settled." I eyed Edith's office, and sure enough, she came trundling out to see what the disturbance was.

"What's this?"

"Santa!" Anya yelled. "He came!"

"But he canceled." Her eyes narrowed as she tried to identify the man behind the fake white beard.

"He's here now," I said brightly.

"And he has a gift for Miss Joy," Steve said with a wink.

"He does?" Edith's tone was unamused, and she stared me down like she had mind-reading powers.

"He does," Steve said smoothly. He winked at my boss, whispering, "No gift for you. I heard you were naughty." She jolted as if she'd been goosed, her cheeks flaming.

"Open it," Steve urged, his attention back on me.

"I will." I began directing the kids toward the carpeted area again, placing the wrapped box on top of a shelf so the kids wouldn't open it for me.

"Come, children," Edith said. "Let's gather on the carpet with Santa."

I stood at the edge of the carpet, waiting to be needed as Steve expertly wrangled the kids into a circle while my boss looked on.

"He's a sweetheart," Emily said, joining me. She smiled and waved at her daughter.

"Steve?" I confirmed.

"He really likes you."

"Oh, I don't know," I said bashfully, feeling a desperation rising within me to pump her for more information, details, anything and everything.

"He thinks very highly of you. In fact, I heard you'll be joining the profession very soon." She gave me a nudge.

"What?" My head snapped away from Santa and the little fantasy that had been playing out, of Steve wrestling sheets onto Max's bed, then tucking him in before joining me for a cup of tea and warm kisses that tasted like chai tea and love.

Emily was smiling at me expectantly. "Steve said you're going back to school for a few classes?"

I'd told only one person that I had applied. One. And he was blabbing all over town when I hadn't even been accepted into the program? That man did not understand the no-meddle rule.

"You chose a great school—they're well-rated for their elementary education program," Emily said. "Do you have your résumé or portfolio ready?"

Portfolio?

"No, not yet."

"Well, when you're ready for a job, let me know."

"There's an opening?" I said. "I mean, it'll probably be a few years before I'm certified..."

"Oh." Emily looked taken aback. "I didn't realize you had that much upgrading to do first."

"That's if I'm accepted into the program."

"Oh, I see. I must have misunderstood." Her cheeks pinked. Emily was no doubt thinking about how I'd sworn up and down that I was going to become a doctor and then hadn't. She'd been a few years ahead of me in school and had been in charge of the yearbook, interviewing students about their future goals. It had been embarrassing having to go back and change mine before it was published. Emily was the kind of woman who made plans, set goals, then burst past them ahead of schedule.

Steve really needed to learn where it was safe to stick his nose. Not only was I feeling as though I had just entered an impromptu interview wholly unprepared, but he'd put Emily in an awkward spot, too.

"I've only just applied." I pulled my sweater sleeves over my hands, wanting to disappear, and struggling not to shoot daggers at Steve who had all the kids cooing over him like it was the most natural thing in the world.

"Do you know which grade you're hoping to teach?" Emily asked, her tone a little less enthusiastic and a bit more professional now.

I shook my head. "No, not yet."

"Well, we're often looking to cover maternity leaves or in need of a substitute teacher here and there. We'll get your name on the list when you're ready."

"Thank you," I said.

Completely unprepared.

I found myself staring at Santa, trying to convince myself that Steve meant well with his meddling, and that I hadn't just ruined my first impression at the one place I most wanted to work—the Christmas Mountain Elementary School.

I CALLED STEVE INTO THE SMALL STAFF ROOM OFF THE BARRICADED playroom. Still dressed as Santa, he was surrounded by shreds of wrapping paper—I'd given up collecting it after he'd suggested the kids rip up every little bit and throw it around like confetti.

Yeah.

He was that guy.

Naturally, the children adored him. There was no fighting or whining, and I figured that we—a.k.a. me, since the other part of today's staff was in her office pretending to work—had about twenty minutes until the bottom dropped out of their good moods.

"What's up?" Steve asked as he joined me in the staff room. He glanced through the window that allowed us to peek out at the kids. The cushion filling out his flat stomach was knocked askew and I reached to straighten it.

"You told Emily I was going back to school?" I asked, trying to make the pillow resemble a bowl full of jelly.

"Yeah. It came up. She sounded excited."

"How did something like that come up?"

"Did you like your Santa gift?"

"I haven't opened it yet." It was still on top of the shelf in the main room.

Steve looked at me expectantly. He didn't understand relationships, did he? There were boundaries to establish, as well as respect, if we were going to make this work. Such as no meddling.

Wait a second. A relationship? Was I seriously considering something more than a casual, my-kid-is-away-for-a-few-days-so-let's-play-around?

I was, wasn't I?

"Santa! Come see my train!" Elias hollered through the window.

Steve raised his eyebrows at me, asking permission. I sighed and gestured toward the door. I wasn't going to get anything helpful from him, anyway. He didn't understand my approach to life.

He turned in the doorway, watching me for a moment.

"No meddling," I said firmly.

"I thought I was just sharing your good news."

"I haven't even been accepted into the program." My frustration exploded. "She was practically interviewing me for a job, thinking I was already looking. It took me off guard, and I gave her the impression that I'm completely oblivious and unprepared and that I don't understand how any of this works!"

Before I could do anything other than suck in a fresh breath to continue my rant, Steve had shut the door again, pulled down his fake Santa beard and was kissing me.

He was trying to soften me up with his wonderful kisses, and sadly, it was working. I was sweating the small stuff again—that was what I did, after all.

He was smiling when he released my limp body, now devoid of anger.

"It's fun being more than a friend," he murmured.

I couldn't help but smile in return—even though I was still upset over how he'd inadvertently set me up.

"I'm sorry I overstepped," he said, his expression sincere. "But you had it coming."

"What? Why?"

"Being awesome and so easy to brag about." He grinned, opening the door, leaving me feeling baffled and slightly charmed.

Moments later he was sprawled on the carpet with the kids, everyone vying for Santa's attention. He was patient with each of them, letting them talk, gently enforcing a take-your-turn-and-don't-interrupt rule. When he sat up, Cynthia, a two-year-old who had sworn off naps, much to the agony of her parents, climbed into his lap and snuggled in, thumb stuck in her mouth. Steve cradled her without a second thought as he played with Elias's train, and in minutes the little girl was asleep despite the hubbub around her. My chest tightened as I watched the sweet scene unfold.

This man... He was very unexpected. Frustrating, but well-intentioned.

An hour or so later parents started coming in to pick up their kids, blasting the entry with cold air and kicking the furnace into high gear. All through the comings and goings, Steve, still in his

Santa costume, held the sleeping toddler. I wanted to wake her so she wouldn't be up all night, but I couldn't make myself budge other than to snap a photo to send to her parents.

Edith appeared at my side. "Staff must adhere to the no-phone policy. When we are with the children that is our number one priority. Distractions cause accidents."

I held up my phone to show her the photo before she fired me on the spot.

Her expression softened. "You should have taken one of all the children with Santa."

"Next year."

She was watching me with a sharp, analyzing look. "That was very nice of Steve to come in."

"It was."

"I hope your relationship doesn't..." She paused as though seeking the right word. "...distract you from watching the children."

She scuttled off before I could react. Had she seen Steve and me kiss in the staff room? She must have, and now feared that his being here might lead me to act unprofessionally. My gaze drifted toward Santa, who was walking toward the entry, offering the sleeping child to her parent.

"I just got Joy's text with the photo," said Cynthia's mother. Her expression was so tender, the love in her eyes worth any grief I got from Edith over Steve's unexpected arrival.

"She napped too long," Edith said, stepping in. "Most kids didn't nap at all. Joy didn't have the heart to wake up Cynthia. I hope she doesn't keep you up half the night."

"That's fine," Cynthia's mom said, giving me a smile that looked more relaxed than any I'd seen in weeks. "She has a few missed naps to make up for. We may actually enjoy an evening without any tantrums."

At the end of my shift, and once everything was set for tomorrow, Steve caught my eye and said, "Ready to go?" He'd been waiting, helping where he could, the costume folded neatly by his jacket, which Emily had dropped off for him.

Outside it was snowing softly, the colored Christmas lights cheerfully lit above us. Steve's hands slipped around my waist and he drew me close.

"Hello," I said, our warm breath creating clouds around us in the dark evening air.

"You're a kind woman."

"Says the man whose arms probably fell asleep along with Cynthia a few hours ago."

"Is letting a child sleep in your arms while you're dressed up as Santa sexy?"

"Maybe."

He kissed me, his lips warm.

I was still in his embrace, considering him, conscious that we were enjoying an embrace anyone could see should they travel down this quiet street. "Not many men would dress up as Santa at a moment's notice."

"Maybe I'm trying to impress a woman."

I couldn't help but blush at the idea that he'd dressed up to impress me. He was smart, knowing the way to my heart was through kids. Although the way he'd acted so naturally, making it all look so easy, made me wonder if kids were his soft spot, too.

"Did my efforts work?" he asked.

"Time will tell."

He appeared crestfallen, and even though I knew he was faking it, I placated him. "You saved the day, and your efforts were very much appreciated."

"It was sweet?"

"Yes."

"Even though unplanned?"

"Yes."

"And even though your boss nearly blew a gasket when the kids didn't all get their naps?"

I chuckled. "Yes. Although she did handle it quite well—keeping it all on the inside instead of exploding all over us."

Steve snugged me closer. "And even though my actions might make you like me more than you want to?"

I laughed. I had no plans to fall in love again, and especially not with someone so frustratingly meddlesome. But I could see that if I wasn't careful, he might just sneak in and steal my heart.

"HEY, GUYS," I SAID, SMILING AT MY PHONE AS MAX AND CALVIN connected to our video chat, a statue of a man on a horse in the background, as well as a fountain and some trees. It looked like a wet and cool evening in Paris.

I'd received an emailed acceptance from the college already, and I was a tangle of nerves.

"What did you do today?" I asked. "Where are you?"

"We're outside!" Max said, coming close enough to Calvin's phone that I could see the shadowy circles of his nostrils.

"We're outside the hotel," Calvin said.

"Grandma's napping and we ate ice cream!"

"And we went to a museum," Calvin added.

"I ate ice cream at the museum."

My heart warmed at his enthusiasm. He was having a good adventure.

"I learned how to say thank-you in French," Max told me. He said something that sounded almost correct, and Calvin winced.

"We're working on our French."

"That's great," I said.

As Max filled me in on their day, Calvin listened with a slightly odd look on his face.

"What's up?" I asked Calvin, when Max began digging through their bag to find the museum map. "How were your meetings?"

"Good. And I just wanted to say that I really appreciate your support, Joy. My mom didn't think you'd be game for me taking Max on this exploratory trip, and it's been really great. We're bonding."

Max popped into view of the screen. "I wore out Grammy." He disappeared again, asking, "Where's the map?"

Calvin mumbled something to Max, then said to me, "Anyway, I really appreciate that you're up for an international move, and how family-focused you are." His smile was warm and kind. I used to do anything for that smile.

I eyed the notes I'd taken about the education classes and the costs of entering college in January. It was all very doable if I got a student loan, as well as a few more hours at the daycare. Assuming I didn't have the cost of moving to France. Calvin said he would cover most of it, since we'd all be moving for him, but I was sure there would be other, unforeseen expenses involved for both of us.

"Today's meetings were positive?" I asked.

"They were."

"When will you know if the project is the right fit?"

"Three to four weeks. It's all still up in the air at the moment. It could be five weeks. Or one." He gave a carefree laugh, unbothered by the unknown and how it was leaving us all in limbo.

The winter semester at the college started in two weeks, but I could take the first several classes toward my degree online, meaning I could be anywhere in the world.

"Has the weather been good?" I asked.

"Nicer than there, that's for sure."

"It's actually quite lovely this morning," I said, thinking how weird it was to have their day ending while mine was just gearing up, due to the eight-hour time difference. I hadn't done much since kissing Santa at work two days ago. Mostly just worked on finishing up Max's room and walking Obi.

"Yeah, but freezing there." Calvin laughed.

"We are in the mountains," I pointed out, feeling oddly defensive.

"I heard a rumor about you," Calvin said, his lips quirked in a bemused fashion.

"A rumor?" My mind immediately went to Steve. Had someone seen us kiss? The song "I Saw Mommy Kissing Santa Claus" started playing in my head.

"I'm not sure what to think of it." Calvin was watching me and I felt on the spot.

"Well, life is unexpected and sometimes... things happen."

"Things happen?"

"Yeah. You know. Out of the blue."

His brow furrowed. "What does that mean?"

"Steve Jorgensen and I might be becoming friends. He—" I caught a glimpse of Max, who was reading his map, and realized I couldn't relay the story of Steve dressing up as Santa. My little boy still held a tenuous belief in Santa Claus. Any day that bubble would burst, but I didn't want to be the one who caused it. I wanted him to believe for as long as possible.

I opened my mouth to mention the helicopter ride, but that felt like the date it had become. I knew Calvin had enjoyed the odd date in the past year, but I felt the need to hold it close to my chest for some reason. Same with movie night.

"For a moment I thought the rumor was true," Calvin said.

I felt my cheeks burn, dreading having to own up to kissing our former co-nemesis.

"But seriously? Why would you go back to school?" Calvin laughed and I nearly choked. "You were so ready to get out of there when I finished my degree that you didn't even finish yours."

"Oh! Um..." My face grew even hotter. I hated the Christmas Mountain grapevine. The rumor of my application had made it to France in less than thirty-six hours. How had I been so naive to believe that I could wait to discuss this with Calvin in person?

"It's true?" He was staring at me, his face slightly pale in the December evening light.

"Um, maybe." I scrunched my nose, trying not to cringe. "I haven't totally decided."

"I thought we were building toward a move to Paris." There was impatience and anger in his tone, to which Max was thankfully oblivious. He held a map up in front of the screen, blocking my view of Calvin.

"There was a statue of a man with a sword and another one of a lady." Max giggled. "Her one private was showing." He lowered the map to gesture to his chest.

"Max, I need to chat with your dad."

Oblivious to my request, Max continued pointing out various things on the map as he chattered a mile a minute. "At the museum there were bathrooms everywhere. And ice cream and doughnuts, but Dad told me only one treat so I had an ice cream, but Grandma bought me a doughnut later because she didn't know. And there was a bench outside, with ducks on a pond. A lady let me feed them her pretzel."

"None of this is for certain yet, Calvin," I said, after giving Max a quick hum of acknowledgment. "France and... everything." I waved a hand and slid my admission notes farther away. "But I..."

"But you what? I thought we were on the same team."

"We are! I can take these courses anywhere." At least the first ones. "I could even study while sitting on that bench feeding the ducks a pretzel."

"An American education degree will be worthless in France. It's a completely different system." Calvin's voice was low and urgent. "You don't need a degree to work where you are, and we're both still paying off our student loans from before."

"I thought you'd like the idea of me expanding my financial independence. And *my* student loans are almost gone." That was one benefit of working so hard during school, as well as taking only a few classes.

"I take good care of you and Max," he said firmly. "I'm good about flexing my schedule or calling my mom to help us when Edith drops a shift in your lap, but that's for *work*."

"And I appreciate that."

His lips had formed a thin line, surprised as he was by the way I was standing up to him. "There's no need to change things. They're working fine."

I sucked in a deep breath and held it to a count of five. I released it and sucked in a second one.

"I don't want to fight, Joy." Calvin shook his head as though disappointed in me.

He wanted me to roll over. Withdraw from the program and lose the application fee, because it was inconvenient for him. My choice could single-handedly put us on separate pages in terms of our goals, making it appear selfish of him if he moved us all to France.

In some ways Calvin and Steve weren't that different. They both wanted me to do things that suited their image of me. Steve wanted me to stretch more. Calvin less.

"What if something happens to your job?" I asked. "Don't you want me to—"

"Are you trying to push me out of your life? Is this about your neighbor? I heard you two are getting close, and that he dressed up as Santa just for you."

"Santa's not real?" Max asked, his eyes round and dark like a wounded cartoon character.

"No, no. Steve was just helping out Santa," I said quickly.

"I thought this guy was your enemy, Joy. This is so weird. It isn't like you." Calvin was shaking his head again.

"I know, okay? I just... I want... I want to be more independent. I want to be able to shoulder the responsibility that befalls me."

Max was staring at us both with wide eyes. We'd never fought in front of him before. Not even while sorting through our divorce.

"Let's talk about this later," I suggested. "Max, just one more sleep for me until I see you again!"

Calvin muttered, "You can bet we'll talk about this later." He pushed himself back on the bench, the phone swaying in his grip. "We have to go. It's late. Goodnight." He ended the call before I could say bye to Max.

I blinked at my phone for a long minute before setting it down. Was this what Steve had been talking about? How everybody liked me being quiet and staying in my place? Calvin obviously wasn't a fan of how I was potentially upending our lives, even if it would be better for both of us overall.

Then again, it was a rather sudden shift for me to go back to school, and I was certain that if I'd been able to break the news to Calvin on my own it would have gone much smoother. Instead, due to Steve's meddling, I'd sideswiped my ex, potentially making everything more difficult.

I finished putting away the paint supplies from Max's room and hurried to the kitchen, where I'd left my phone. I had an idea how I could help convince Calvin that college was a good idea. He'd wanted me to get a degree originally, so what I needed was for him to see why returning to complete it was smart. The first step I needed to take was to enlist the rumor mill's support, and for everyone to understand that I wasn't doing this for selfish reasons—it was for Max and myself. And, I supposed, Calvin, too. If I could get people to see that, then maybe they could help me convince Calvin that this was the best thing for our family even if the timing was poor in regards to his opportunity in France.

I dialed my mom, knowing I could trust her conservative,

thoughtful approach to life decisions. If I was being rash, she'd set me straight.

"Mom?" I said, when the phone stopped ringing on the other end but I was met by silence.

"Joy? Sorry. I dropped my phone. These cellular things are so hard to grip. Why don't you call my home number?"

"What did you do today?" I asked.

"How are you doing?"

"Fine. Why?"

"Max has been gone for almost a week now."

"I just talked to them. They'll be home really late tomorrow."

"And?"

"They went to a museum."

"Hmm. I heard something."

"About Max?" My heart started racing.

"What's wrong with Max?" she squeaked. I could hear the worst-case-scenario panic rising in her voice. My mother liked living in a small town because nothing big or scary ever happened. Or at least very rarely.

"He's fine. You said you heard something."

"It was about you."

My mind raced through the past few days and the possible things she could have heard. Would it be the same rumor that had reached Calvin about school, or would it be the one about Steve?

"Jan at the grocery store said you're going back to school." Jan was a longtime gossip, due to supersede Judith Smith once the retired woman met her maker. "I told her you weren't, because why would you do that?" There was humor in her voice.

"I'm considering some upgrading so I can teach elementary school."

"But you're happy at Little Comets?"

Happy. That word just kept coming up, didn't it?

"I could use more hours."

"I'm sure Edith could give you more if you just asked." My mom paused a beat, then added, "I thought you wanted to be home for Max?"

"If I was a teacher I'd have the same holidays, as well as a retirement fund, health insurance and a better income."

Mom gave a sympathetic huff, then said, "You know we love you just the way you are. You don't have to go back to school and get a big career for us to be proud of you."

"I know."

"Sometimes we need to be happy with what we have."

Guilt edged at me. Was I asking too much? I knew Carol and Cassandra would say I wasn't, and I trusted them—as well as Steve, who seemed to be right more often than not.

"I want more financial security for us," I said. "This is about bettering our lives."

"But you have Calvin..." My mom honestly believed I had the best thing going—child support and a job that allowed me to be home with Max as much as I needed. But she'd also expressed quite a bit of confusion over the divorce, since Calvin and I were obviously still good friends. She didn't seem to fully understand that the boundaries between Calvin and me were growing—and that it was healthy for them to do so.

"I don't have Calvin." My tone was hard, unforgiving. I had been playing with a nicely wrapped box of cookies I'd made as a just-in-case gift should I need something last-minute, and I set them down on the counter with a thunk.

Calvin was back in the world of dating. And as of this week, so was I. Surely if one of us started a new family the courts would decide he didn't need to—or couldn't afford to—pay as much in the way of support. And if he moved to France, then what? My costs would go up as I helped send Max back and forth across the Atlantic.

My jaw dropped. Was I really considering putting my foot

down and not moving? Was I going to let my little boy live thousands of miles away from me?

My head started to pound like I'd been leaped on by a toddler and received an inadvertent head-butt.

"I'm having to depend on Calvin a lot," I said slowly, "and I shouldn't have to do that. I'm an adult."

"But he's Max's father. That's his responsibility. You hold him to that!"

"Calvin does just fine by us, but child support won't last forever. I'll want to retire someday. What if one of us remarries?"

My mom gave a hum of understanding. "Judith said she saw you talking to that boy you used to come home all upset about in high school. You were never happy with your life after the two of you started partnering in chemistry. He brought out the wild side in you."

"The wild side?"

"That pig incident. I know he was behind it. Don't think I didn't see him across from the police station when we brought you home. Judith warned me that something was up, with the two of you living right next door to each other now, but I didn't believe it." She made a tsking noise.

"Mom, none of this is because of Steve." The pounding in my head was not improving, especially since my words felt like a lie. I found myself pushing aside my curtains, glancing at the dark house next door. "You know the pigs had nothing to do with him. He was there to bail me out."

My mother sighed. "Joy, you've always wanted so much. Medical school and now this. Not everyone has to get a degree, you know. And it's going to be difficult going back to school with a young boy at home."

I'd find a way. I had to. I was Max's mom, and it was my job to figure things out. And I knew I'd have Steve on my side. He believed I could do this, and I trusted him—even though he failed to understand why I hadn't continued on to medical school despite the obstacles.

That man had a way of turning my life inside out. Case in point, I was currently arguing with my mother, with her securely in my old role and saying everything I had spouted to Steve as excuses only days earlier. How had things changed so quickly that I now disagreed with her, as well as resented Calvin's blowback?

"Is that man making you feel like you're not good enough, Joy?"

"No. He's helping me see a way to be the person I *want* to be. One who can depend on herself. Someone who doesn't have to go to her ex-husband if her roof starts leaking. Someone who can offer the things her son needs. I managed school once, and I'll manage it again," I said, in a tone I very rarely used with my mom. "I am doing this. I'm going back to school. No matter what."

CHAPTER 8

*M*ax was coming home tonight, and I had been watching the clock since before dawn, waiting for it to be time to make the late-night drive to the airport to pick him up. Would Calvin and Max return to Christmas Mountain totally in love with France and eager to go back immediately? Or would they be happy to stay here? My mind was a mess of questions, so when Edith called to see if I could cover the last few hours of Tonya's shift, as she'd gone home sick, I was all-in.

When my shift ended, I gathered up my coat, but was called in to Edith's small office just off the kids' playroom. I had the next four days off to celebrate Christmas, as the daycare was closed, but I was prepared to say yes if she needed me to take on more hours once it opened again.

As I sat across from her, I took in the grim line of her mouth and realized I wasn't about to be granted a larger paycheck this month due to an increase in hours. Nope. I was fairly certain it would be a lecture about having my boyfriend visit me at work—which was what she'd transformed Steve's Santa stunt into since she'd seen us kiss. It didn't matter that I had denied the relationship status. In fact, I hadn't even seen Steve since the Santa kiss.

He was busy running pre-Christmas tours, and I was subtly and successfully avoiding him while dropping the news around town that I was enrolled in some online courses to upgrade my skills.

Even though Steve and I had spent only a few days together, it felt odd not hanging out with him, as well as sharing the news that I'd secured a student loan, and was officially due to start two online courses in January.

"I've been hearing things," Edith said from behind her desk.

"Oh?" I wasn't sure if this was about me or about the daycare. With her it could be anything.

She licked her lips and leaned forward, tapping the surface of her desk as though unsure what to say. Whatever it was, it wasn't great.

I found myself leaning forward as well.

"I hope that you'll tender your resignation in a timely manner so I can find a suitable replacement."

I jolted backward in the chair. "What?"

"I had hoped that I'd earned enough trust and respect that you'd give me advance notice—more than the required two weeks. It is difficult to find qualified staff." She had begun arranging papers, and now whacked them into a neat pile. "I've drawn up a draft of the ad for the job. I just need to know the start date for the new recruit."

Her eyes met mine and I felt my spine give way.

"But why?" If I wasn't working here, I wasn't sure what would happen with my student loan. Could I find a new job in time? "I mean... I'm not leaving. Am I fired?"

"Steve told me you're going back to school in the city."

Steve. That no-meddling rule really gave him comprehension issues, didn't it?

"I'm just taking some online classes in my free time. From home." Why hadn't the grapevine told her that part of the story? I'd even told Judith and Jan, in hopes of the word spreading a bit faster.

"Courses so you can become a teacher," Edith stated, that grim furrow still bending her eyebrows downward.

"Yes. Once I've completed the classes I'll be able to take my state certification tests."

"When?"

"A year, maybe two."

She relaxed into her chair. "You still plan to work here full-time until then?"

I slid to the edge of my seat. "I'd love full-time hours. Do you need me to get you Max's school schedule for January? I believe he has only one Friday off, near the end of the month."

She caught herself, sitting straighter. "I'm not sure I can offer more hours at this time." She lined her pens up like they were darts she might need to throw at someone. "But I need to know you'll be available to work when I need you to."

"Of course. Nothing will change in that regard." I crossed my fingers like Max did when he told a fib. I could already foresee that the future classes I had to take on campus were going to be a problem. As was the in-the-classroom practicum I'd be doing toward the end of my degree. Assuming, of course, that I didn't find myself living in France.

"Good. I can't flex on both your course work needs and your motherhood needs."

I bit my tongue so I didn't say that with the few hours she was giving me I was certain I could flex more than a yoga teacher and still be fine.

"I'll be available when you need me." I stood. "Just like I always have been. And I'm also going to need more hours. I know Tonya needs them, but so do I."

Edith stood as well, her eyes drilling into mine. "When you're here with the children, I expect you to be fully here."

"I will be, just like always." I tried for a smile, but it felt forced and I let it go.

"You may have to make some sacrifices, Joy." She looked

down, her lips pursed for a moment as she tapped one of the pens in her lineup. "I'll see what I can do about your hours, but remember that we can't have everything we want." She solidly met my gaze and I nodded, feeling as though I'd just accomplished a small win in a long battle.

"Of course." If anyone knew that, it was the old Joy. The new Joy? Well, she was already tweaking that belief.

I ANSWERED THE DOOR AFTER WORK, SHUSHING OBI, WHO WAS going slightly wild.

"Say it, don't spray it," I muttered, wiping his spittle off the doorknob. He finally calmed down when he saw it was Madia Benson, the local real estate agent who'd been a few grades behind me. She'd been totally in love with volleyball, always practicing in the school hallways.

"Hi, Joy. Merry Christmas."

"Merry Christmas." I pulled Obi farther from the door as he strained to sniff her gorgeous brown leather boots. He had a thing for gnawing on leather, and I was pretty sure I couldn't afford replacements—even if Edith did start giving me more hours.

"I was just in the neighborhood and thought I'd drop off my card," Madia trilled.

I took her business card, feeling confused. She'd helped me find this home, and we were already friends on every form of social media we belonged to and had been on the same volleyball team in middle school. In other words, I knew where to find her.

"Spring is the optimal time for selling, but as soon as you're ready I can help you get this place on the market. We can work together on how to get the most from a potential buyer, with some tricks such as decluttering and staging a few rooms so it sells faster. I do have a family looking for a small starter home right now, though. There's not a lot in this price range available. Do you want me to set something up? I'm sure you're eager to get moving and reclaim your down payment."

"I'm sorry?"

"I heard you're moving to the city to go back to school in January." Her smile was bright. Innocent. "Or to France maybe?" she said, her tone becoming uncertain. "I just assumed that you'd want to sell."

"I'm taking online courses, and we don't know about France yet." I tried not to grit my teeth. "Things are a bit up in the air with that."

"Oh." Madia looked at the card I'd crushed in my fist. "Well, I think it's great that you're going back to school. You'll be a great teacher."

"Thank you."

"If you need anything, you know where to find me." She began backing down the steps. "Merry Christmas!"

As soon as she'd pulled away I was in my boots and coat, pounding on Steve's door.

"Joy!" His smile was huge until he caught my stormy expression.

"Thanks a lot." I pushed my way inside his entry.

"Uh, you're welcome?" He scratched the back of his head and gave me what was likely supposed to be a confused look.

"Why does the entire town think I'm moving to the city? And how did Calvin know I'd applied for school before I even had a chance to tell him?" I marched closer, not caring that my boots were dropping snow onto Steve's clean, dry floors. "Why does my boss think I'm resigning? Why did Madia Benson just pop by to discuss putting my house on the market?"

This kind of uncertainty was going to be hard on Max, and I needed to get the town under control before he returned. It was bad enough that France was a possibility. He'd weathered the divorce well, but this, I feared, would be too much uncertainty and change for a small boy.

"They're proud of you," Steve said. "They want to help you follow your dreams."

I closed my eyes, trying to remain focused. I'd wanted support. I'd wanted the town to understand why I needed to do this. But I'd told everyone I was taking online courses. Online! Not moving.

So why did people think I was moving? Steve.

My quest to help Calvin see that me returning to school was a smart move was beginning to feel like a campaign. One where I was undermining his desire to strike out fresh in France.

"What if something goes wrong with getting this degree? I was going to become a doctor and I didn't. What if I don't make it? What if life happens?"

"You'll make it."

"I know I will, but you need to stop meddling and trying to make my life into what you think it should be. I'm taking classes while living here in Christmas Mountain. I'm not moving."

"I know."

"You told Edith I'm taking classes in the city!"

"I didn't say you were moving."

Then why had she been ready to start advertising my job? Immediately.

I tried to calm myself. It made sense that people assumed I would move to the city to complete my degree, just as Calvin and I had years ago. It wasn't all Steve's fault. But we needed to set some ground rules.

"If you and I are going to humor the idea that we might have a chance, I need to be enough for you just the way I am. As I am at this very second in time. A single mom subsisting just above the poverty level, happily living in a small town. Not some woman taking on the world and grand adventures, just waiting to break out into something huge."

Steve stepped back, crossing his strong arms.

"I'm a quiet people pleaser, Steve. Not everyone needs to be the CFO of a large company in order to be happy or feel satisfied with their life."

"I didn't say they do." His jaw was tight now, as was his voice.

"It's implied. I need to be with someone who doesn't push the whole town into... into whatever they're thinking and saying. I'm taking *online classes*."

"They're not just online classes."

"I need someone who will support me if I change my mind and stay working in a daycare. I don't need you..." I had run out of words and I gestured helplessly. I liked the support, but not the semi-constant interference.

"Meddling? Supporting you? Helping to clear a path?"

"Yes! And creating misunderstandings."

"So you'd rather do this alone, and not let others help you in case you fail—which you won't."

"Yes! No." I didn't know anymore. I only knew that Steve was muddying the waters and causing things to spin out of control for me. Returning to school was scary enough as it was.

"I need to keep things normal," I said, fighting to remain calm. "As they are. I have a little boy to consider."

"You'd rather I help convince you that your current life is just fine, and that there isn't more to want," Steve said, his focus on my jacket's undone zipper rather than on my face. "That it's perfectly fine and acceptable to be locked into a life where you pretend to be happy, struggling to subsist on handouts from your ex?"

"Leave Calvin out of this."

"I can't." He finally met my eyes, a sad resolve settling into his. "He's a part of your life, and he's a part of what is holding you back from being you."

"I'm already me!"

"There's only one woman I want to be with, Joy, and from

what I'm hearing, she's too afraid to stand up and be who she is and speak up for what she wants."

"Steve…" I warned.

"No. You're not brave enough to be the woman I see inside of you, and I won't be with anyone but her."

It was nearly Christmas Eve Day; it was so late as I stood in the arrivals area of the airport, hands stuffed deep into my pockets while I waited for Calvin and Max. To say I was still frustrated with Steve was an understatement. Maybe he'd move away. Forever.

To my left someone held up a sign that said Luke Cohen and Emma Carrington, people I didn't know, but names that seemed oddly familiar. There were only a few of us waiting for the small plane that was coming in from Seattle, making the sign unnecessary.

Max, Calvin and his mother had taken three different flights to get from Paris to our neck of the woods, and I had a strong feeling Max would be exhausted, jet-lagged and basically as unhappy as a poked bear.

I was so excited to see him my bladder had kicked into overdrive, even though I'd had nothing to drink for hours.

Max and Calvin returning could allow me to pretend everything in my life was back as it should be. They were home. Nobody was going anywhere right away. We would all do our own thing tomorrow, then enjoy Christmas Day together. There was no Steve pushing me, telling me to be some woman I wasn't so he could love me. I was back to me. Joy Evans ensconced in the quiet life I loved.

The life that now somehow felt as though something was missing from it.

I scoffed at myself. All that was missing was conflict with

pushy Steve. How silly was I? I'd pegged him early on as unable to go the distance, and yet I'd allowed my hopes to climb. But at least I hadn't dragged Max into it. In the coming days he was going to be confused enough, with everyone asking me about school, moving and France. The poor boy wouldn't know if his parents were coming or going, and my job would be to show him everything in his life was stable. And that was easier without Steve.

Calvin and Max came through the opaque glass security doors, looking grim and fed up with each other. Calvin had Max's hand, and Max was trying to go limp on him, making his knees buckle every time Calvin tried to make him stand.

"Let's go," he said to Max. "There's Mom."

Calvin looked relieved to get within range of me, practically dragging our son into my open arms. Max wound himself around me as my mother-in-law ignored the whole scene, moving to the conveyor belt, where suitcases had yet to appear.

Max whined, "I'm tired."

"I know, sweetie." I kissed his cheek. "I missed you." I hugged him tightly, then turned to Calvin. "How was the trip?"

"Long. We're jet-lagged." Calvin pushed a hand through his hair. He stepped back, no doubt done with parenting our wiped-out boy.

I whispered in Max's ear, "It's almost Christmas!"

He didn't respond. I wasn't sure if he was asleep or just ignoring me. Although his weight hadn't suddenly amplified, which meant he was likely still conscious. I did some quick mental math. Paris was eight hours ahead, meaning they were about ready for breakfast.

"Are you hungry?"

Max shook his head.

"You're going to need to walk." I tried to set him down, but he refused to unhook his legs from around my hips.

My mother-in-law had found her suitcase and was already

trucking ahead, coming to a halt at the exit. With Max still in my arms, I walked beside Calvin, who had plucked up the rest of the bags.

"Things went okay?" I tipped my head toward his mom.

Calvin's jaw tightened, but he didn't offer anything other than, "Things went fine."

He was still such a poor liar. He'd obviously done or said something his mother disagreed with. The good news for him was that she always forgave him almost immediately and would soon return to doting on him.

"Any word on a piano?" I asked Calvin as we walked across the almost empty corridor toward the doors.

"Joy, I'm tired."

"I know. It's just that it's basically already Christmas Eve, and for the extravaganza I—"

"It's Christmas. How will I get a piano in time?"

"I just thought maybe you'd had a line on something even though you were away."

"I texted you before I left."

"You did. I was just checking, in case." I really hoped Steve had managed to replace the dead piano key, and that he didn't hold a grudge that would cause him to abandon the project because we'd fought.

"Did they make you a job offer?" I asked, awkwardly shifting Max's weight.

"Mom, we're out this way," Calvin said.

"Actually, I parked this way," I said, nodding in a different direction. "Max? Can you walk? It's slippery out and I don't want to fall."

He shook his head in the crook of my neck.

"Please." I lowered my arms, causing him to slide down to his feet.

If this was what it was going to be like after each trip to France, the situation would be torture for all of us.

Once on the highway, I asked my passengers how Disneyland Paris had been, assuming Calvin's lack of reply about the job meant he didn't know and didn't want to speculate.

"It was fine," Calvin answered. I could hear his mother snoring in the backseat already, Max likely asleep as well, since he didn't pipe up.

"I registered for two online classes," I said. "They start the first week in January."

Calvin sighed. "Joy, we were going to discuss this once I was home."

"Then now's the time, I guess. I might need to switch the odd day with you when it comes time to study for exams."

"*Before* you registered," he said, his tone tight.

"I couldn't wait."

"Why? Why all of this sudden need? It's hardly the moment to overextend yourself financially or in regards to your time. How are we going to swing you going back to school in the city, when we're raising a boy in two separate households hours away from there?"

"There is no 'we'," I snapped. "And frankly, I'm not up to hearing about how my life is going to inconvenience yours. You should be happy I'm seeking this out. It'll give us both more freedom, independence, and it will be better for Max in the long run."

We drove the rest of the way to Christmas Mountain in silence.

I dropped off Calvin's mom first, then pulled up outside Calvin's place. When I began unloading Max, who was now bounding with energy, Calvin said, "I thought he could stay with you tonight."

It was around two in the morning and Max's body was geared up like it was 10:00 a.m.—which it was in Paris. That meant he was ready to go at his day full-throttle, and I'd yet to fall asleep.

"Maybe the two of you should stay here, take a nap this afternoon, then get up for a few hours."

I coaxed Max out of the car and put his hand in Calvin's. "You need to get yourselves back on local time." I smiled as Max threw himself down in the snow and made a snow angel.

"I can see stars!" he said with glee. "I'm up past my bedtime!"

"What?" Calvin asked me, looking dazed. "But I really need some rest."

"I know. So does Max. So do I." I backed away, my heart breaking at possibly giving up Max on what should be my day with him. But I could see it in my mind as clearly as if it was happening. Calvin would go take care of himself, and I'd be up all night with a boy whose body thought it was morning. I'd exhaust myself before Christmas and the extravaganza, moving through the two occasions like a zombie so Calvin could recover faster, when it had been his choice to put himself through this in the first place. Then he'd boast about how it was nothing, taking our boy back and forth through several time zones.

I crouched down to where Max was still in the snow. "I love you, Max. I'm going to go home and sleep, since it's my bedtime. You can come over to our house in the morning, okay?"

Max leaped into my arms, giving me a big hug and a kiss. "I love you, Mom."

"Love you, too. See you guys tomorrow."

"Joy!" Calvin gaped at me as I backed away.

I hurried to my car before I changed my mind, my legs trembling from the fact that I'd finally stood up for myself, and for what I wanted. What I needed.

CHAPTER 9

I was waiting off to the side of the stage area in the community center with my old friends Ash, Morgan, Emma, Carol, Faith and Lexi, ready to perform our song. We were up next and I felt jittery. Getting up onstage was always the hardest part. But once my fingers hit the keys everything else always fell away. I hoped it would stay true for me again tonight in the packed building.

As the group ahead of us bowed and accepted their applause I found Max in the crowd. I wiggled my fingers at him, and he smiled and waved back with an enthusiasm that made me feel special. He'd had quite a few naps since returning, and was getting over his jet lag. He was mostly back to his regular self, swinging his legs in the chair beside his dad. Calvin saw me and gave a smile and nod, the night's program curled in his hands. Next year or the year after would the empty seat beside him that was reserved for me be filled by someone new? Or would he be off in France, despite the rumors I'd heard from Judith while walking Obi yesterday evening, about Calvin not being impressed with the agency that was currently recruiting him?

Carol nudged me. It was time to go onstage, our tribute to

Melody King having been announced. My heart rate increased as I made my way to the piano. I pulled in a breath or two as I set out my music. I had the song memorized, and the sheets of music were more of a security blanket in case I lost my place or mentally blanked out.

The keys before me were cleaner than they'd been a few days ago, and I stroked one of them as I inhaled the instrument's old-wood-and-polish smell. It reminded me of my piano at home, the same brand of polish having been rubbed into its old, lacquered cabinet. Even the brass pedals had been polished, giving them a glorious shine. Someone had given this upright piano some love, and I knew it hadn't been the caretaker, Michelle. Before I realized it, I was looking over my shoulder, seeking out a familiar set of eyes.

I found them in the same place I had when I was seventeen. Steve was lounging against the back wall, hands in his jeans pockets, waiting, watching, his expression unreadable. I mouthed a *thank you,* receiving a nod.

The girls were waiting for me to start and I sucked in a breath and lowered my hands to the keys. As my fingers began to dance, the character of the instrument charmed me with its familiarity. It was the same piano I'd played as a teen, and I felt a swell of gratitude at Steve's persistence in repairing it instead of replacing it. His effort and care had brought out the beauty in the wood grains, taking its battered old appearance and flaws and transforming them into something to admire. Even the silent key rang true tonight, having found its voice in a gentle repair. Steve had seen this piano's potential, just like he had my own. He was a man who noticed things that were swimming along below the surface, and he was unrelenting about having his opinion about them taken into account.

I finished "I'll Be Home for Christmas," having been barely aware of playing. The girls took a bow as the audience wiped at tears, and I joined them before mutely walking offstage. The girls and I wordlessly gathered into a circle off to the side, sharing hugs.

"To Ms. King," we whispered, our voices thick with grief.

As the next performance began, we melted back into the audience, joining our families. I was supposed to sit beside Calvin and Max, but the seat that had been saved was now filled by the flirty gal Emma had warned me about from the lodge at Blacktail Mountain. Max was pouting, arms crossed, and I considered waving him out of the row to come stand with me along the back wall with Steve, but when I glanced Steve's way, his familiar form had vanished, just like it had at the end of our song all those years ago when we were teens.

Instead, I stood alone along the side wall, hands behind my back as the last of the night's performers took to the stage.

When the last performance finished, I began moving toward the door to meet up with Calvin and Max, my jobs with the community center's silent auction having been completed earlier. It felt odd being here without Ms. King, and to know that I was part of the next generation tasked with helping carry on her memory as well as the town's traditions.

My parents drifted by, giving me hugs and well wishes before heading out into the dark night.

Max launched into me and I ruffled his hair, wishing it was my night to have him. It felt as though Calvin had had him for so long with the trip, and now jet lag recovery. I knew it would even out in the long run, and I was grateful Calvin had taken him, but it still made me feel as though I was losing out, even though Calvin and Max had come over to my house for Christmas morning.

"You played well," Calvin said. His posture became slightly awkward. "Did Steve get you a new piano?"

I shook my head. "He just brought out the best in this one."

Calvin pushed a hand partly through his hair, his gaze on my boots. When he looked up, he let out the breath he'd been holding. "I think he's also brought out the best in some other things, too."

"What do you mean?"

"I mean..." Calvin paused, the words not coming easily to him. "You seem different."

"I'm not."

"A few weeks ago you wouldn't have decided to go back to school." He caught my sharp inhalation, and as if afraid I was going to light into him, added quickly, "It's good. I like it. And you're right to want more for yourself. And... I'll help you in any way I can. I'm sorry I wasn't more supportive when you told me about going back."

"You already help me more than you should."

"No." It was his turn to shake his head. "We were partners, and just because we're no longer together doesn't mean I get to renege on obligations."

Obligations. Somehow that was what I'd become to him. It was an unfortunate word choice, but I understood his intended sentiment. He was here and had my back, just like I'd had his during our school years. It wasn't his fault—or mine—that our love hadn't lasted.

"You're a good man," I whispered, barely trusting my voice.

"I could be better."

"We could all be better."

We smiled and shared Christmas greetings with the town mayor, Harriet Millar, as she hobbled by with her walker, her family following in a quiet procession of head nods as they moved past us and out into the cold winter night.

"I said no to France," Calvin murmured. We were still standing by the door, and the way he said it was almost like it was directed at the departing Millars rather than to me.

"Why?"

"It was asking too much."

"The job was?"

"No, moving to France was asking too much of all of us." He glanced toward his mom, who was chatting with her husband and Miles Wilson, now recovered from his bout with the flu. "I was being selfish."

The tension that had been slowly weaving through me over the past few days, tightening as it wound around me, suddenly unspooled, leaving me feeling free. We were staying put. The only disruption in the New Year would be me spending a bit more time behind textbooks and my laptop.

"Thank you."

The community center was almost empty now, the chairs already stacked and put away. The silent auction organizers had closed and collected the bidding sheets so they could contact the winners, and the three of us shifted closer to the door, where we'd part ways. I zipped my coat up to my chin, then told Max to zip up his as well.

We stood quietly, a sadness befalling me. A woman who'd just been granted a reprieve from another move, this one international, and was faced with the opportunity to pursue her chosen degree, with support from her ex, should feel a bit more joyful than I was, shouldn't she? Was it simply because Christmas was now over? The dinners done? The extravaganza and community events wrapped up?

Or was it something else? Something more Steve-related? Because truthfully, I missed him, and even his meddlesome ways. He wasn't perfect, and I wasn't, either. But together... we were better.

I sighed, promising myself I'd work through that little revelation later on tonight, when I was alone.

"You'll tell me if you need anything for school?" Calvin asked, lightly touching my sleeve.

"I'll need extra child care from time to time."

Calvin nodded, a slight smile haunting his lips. "A few weeks ago you wouldn't have. You're—"

"I'm the same," I insisted.

"No. This is good." There was affection and approval in his gaze. "I like that you're standing up for what you need—even if it means you're going to be busting my chops a lot more." He winked before I could get upset, then reached out to touch my sleeve again, saying softly, "It looks good on you."

"Thank you."

Calvin tipped his head toward the exit, and I peeked through the doorway. Steve was waiting just outside on the steps, and my heart did one of those skips that would alarm a cardiologist.

"I don't know what happened that made you two friends, but I think it's good, too." There was that flicker of a smile from Calvin again. It felt like a part of each of us was saying goodbye again. And in a way, like we were still figuring out how to grow up, too.

"Go say hi." Calvin gave me a nudge when my shyness caused me to hesitate. He smiled, and suddenly he was that teenage boy I had wanted to win over. The boy who I believed would always be on my side.

In some ways, maybe he still was.

STEVE WAS LEANING AGAINST THE RAILING, HANDS IN HIS POCKETS, when Calvin, Max and I left the community center. He looked handsome, calm and somehow sure of himself despite our tough words two nights ago.

"Goodnight, Joy," Calvin said, ushering Max down the steps as he gave Steve a nod of acknowledgment. "Steve."

"Calvin," he replied, nodding in turn. He put a hand out for Max to high-five on his way by. "Hey, little man." Max jumped, meeting Steve's hand with his own.

"Hey, big man!" he chirped.

I stopped on the top step as my family continued on.

"Merry Christmas," I said to Steve.

"Was the piano okay?"

"Someone brought out the best in it." I dared myself to meet his eyes so he'd understand I was putting myself out there, and that I appreciated his gesture. "I was ready to discard it, but I was wrong."

"That's funny." He gave me a crooked smile, his head down so he could give me one of those carefree, casual looks that were kind of sexy if I let myself think about it.

Which I didn't. At least not too much, since he seemed to be laughing at me.

"How's that?" I had my arms crossed, but tried to force myself not to get riled up.

"I was wrong, too."

"You were?" I put a palm on my chest as my heart gave an extra thump. Man, if I hung out around Steve much more I was going to have to book an appointment with a cardiologist.

He shifted, moving away from the railing. Toward me. "I was wrong about you."

"What?" I sounded breathless. If I didn't know this was a well-known Steve Effect I'd have my lungs checked out, too.

"I judged you for caring about others. And you're right. I saw my mother in you. You share a lot of her traits. I feared that you were getting the raw end of a bargain. I care about you, Joy."

"I care about you, too."

"That isn't what I was hoping to hear."

"What?" My heart dropped.

"Maybe I should say it first." His fingers found mine, entwining our hands together. "I love you, Joy."

Okay, call back the cardiologist; this man was going to give me a heart attack tonight.

"I want the best for you, and I hope that somehow, even though I'm just some guy who annoys you, that you will find room for me in your life."

I held back for a moment, then gave up and threw my arms

around him. I nestled my face against his neck and just breathed him in, enjoying the feel of his strong arms wrapped around me.

Steve Jorgensen loved me. Me! Joy Evans. The object of his judgment. Because he wanted good things for me.

"Does this hug mean I can stick around and continue to be a meddling pain in your butt?"

I slid out of his arms and stood in front of him. "I thought you were going to try and reform?"

"Nope. You have to love me just the way I am, because most of the time I'm right."

"Good. Don't change a single thing about your meddlesome, bratty self."

He ran the pad of his index finger down my nose, then gave it a light tap. "And why should I stay like this and not reform?" He had a mischievous twinkle in his eye as though he figured I was about to walk into a well-laid trap.

"Because I love you, you big, nosy, bossy know-it-all. You were right about my life." I let out a quick, loud sigh. "And you pushed me to start making some changes. They're small and potentially disruptive, but I'm fairly sure they'll pay off." I finished huffing at him and met his eyes. "And I hope that you will be here to see them."

"I will be," he said, sliding his arms around my waist.

I splayed my hands against his chest. "But you also need to know that I am not some big adventure. I like living here, and I like being a mom and having things just so."

"You don't know me very well, do you?" He mimicked my bemused smile, and said, "You are all the adventure I need. Plus more adventure than you realize in the way you keep me on my toes all the time."

I laughed, then tipped my head to the side, giving him my best Mom-is-not-impressed look, so he'd know I was being serious.

"Sometimes, Joy," he said in a confiding tone, "a man roams the earth and does crazy things like jumping out of planes because there is no one waiting for him at home. There's no one to hold his hand and snuggle against him while watching some cheesy romantic movie. There's no one lighting up when he walks in the door. No one to share his secrets and dreams with. And so he keeps looking. Keeps going on these adventures, trying to chase away the emptiness inside. Taking risks and trying to find a way to light up that dark void."

He cupped my hands between his, whispering, "Joy Evans, you chase away my emptiness. You challenge me to think differently, and you are all the adventure a man like me will ever need."

My eyes grew damp and my heart felt about eight million times too large for my body. It was the most brilliant, wonderful feeling in the world.

"I don't believe you," I whispered huskily.

"Believe me. Because I am here to stay. I love you, Joy."

"I love you, too, Steve Jorgensen."

We met each other's eyes and burst out laughing. Before long we were clutching our sides, helpless and unable to breathe. I looked at him and pointed, and our laughter started up all over again.

"Can I lock up?" Michelle asked, after popping her head out the door and giving us a skeptical look.

We burst out laughing again and I nodded, unable to speak. She closed the door behind us.

"Who would have ever thought?" I said, gesturing to Steve, then myself, leaning against him for support when my laughter ebbed again.

"I kind of had a suspicion."

Before I could ask when it had started, he kissed me, and I forgot about everything but this man standing in the cold, keeping me warm, safe and loved.

CHAPTER 10

Steve and I walked home from the extravaganza, Christmas lights throughout town illuminating our way. We held hands, the surety of him beside me all that I needed.

"You were right," I said. "The town is very supportive of me going back to school. Even Calvin's come around, and my friends have offered to babysit for me during exams." I knew they would be there for me when I needed them. Just like Calvin would be. But, hopefully, soon I wouldn't need him as much as I had in the past, leaving him free to live his new post-Joy life, as I would be free to live mine.

"I'm often right," Steve said.

As we drew close to our homes, I asked, "Whose red truck is that in your driveway?"

"My dad's." Steve dropped my hand, pushing his deep into his coat pockets. "He came up from Kalispell along with my brother to deep-fry a turkey."

"How did that go?"

"Good. He's sleeping off his annual turkey-induced coma. I came over to see if you wanted to join us for supper, but you weren't home."

"Thanks. I was at my parents'."

"How did Max like his room? Has he seen it yet?"

"He loves it. Especially the *Star Wars* poster." I added wryly, "In fact, I probably could have saved myself some time and just bought a bunch of posters instead of painting."

"I'm glad." There was a pause. "Well," Steve said, leaning in to kiss my cheek. "Merry Christmas."

I put my hands on my hips and gave him a look. When he frowned in confusion I tapped my lips. "Put it here, mister."

He complied and I slipped my arms around his neck, bringing him in for a wonderful Christmas kiss.

"I have a gift for you," I said.

"Another pocketknife?"

I gave him a sharp look. "What?" He'd known that secret Santa gift was from me?

He smiled, that same generous, warm one that made me feel like I'd found my home. "I knew it was from you."

"You did?"

"It's something I've always treasured. Thank you."

"You're welcome."

"I've always wondered, though. Why give me such a nice gift when I was a thorn in your side?"

"It just felt right."

We stared at each other for a long moment. There was still so much to discover with this man. So much I had assumed incorrectly, and needed to alter. I had a hunch he felt the same way about me.

"What's your gift?" he asked.

"It's inside." We let ourselves in, and I grabbed the emergency gift I'd made just in case I needed to reciprocate for an unexpected offering. It was the last of two presents under my tree. The other was the gift from him, when he played Santa at Little Comets. Holding the box of baking, I wondered why I hadn't considered getting something special for Steve. Maybe it was all the fighting? All the denial I had steeped myself in when it came to how attracted I was to him?

He slipped off his boots to follow me into the living room, where he shifted uncomfortably.

"What's up?" I asked.

"I talked to my dad." He let out a breath, and said quickly, "My mom was sick before she left her job at Cohen's. She quit and stayed home so she could be with us, because she knew her days were numbered. She wanted to spend her best ones with us." He swallowed hard.

I gave his arm a squeeze, and his lips twisted into a pained smile, full of grief.

"I'm glad she did," I said.

"I can't believe I thought her illness had to do with us and giving up her dreams." Steve shook his head, no doubt regretting so many of his actions, which had been fueled by the false facts around his mother's last days.

"I'm glad you talked to your dad about it."

Steve pushed a hand through his hair, his chest expanding. "He felt awful that I'd gotten it all wrong."

"Are you okay?"

"Yeah." He pulled me into his arms and rested his head on mine. "I'm sorry I took it out on you."

"Don't be. You helped shape me into who I am today, and I like who I am."

He released me. "So do I."

I handed him the wrapped box of cookies. "It's not much."

He took it, looking at me for a long moment. "How do I deserve you?"

I laughed and gestured to the gift. "Open it."

He did so, then smiled. "I told my dad about these. I look forward to returning the container and using it as an excuse to come over to kiss you goodnight."

"Well, I'd better bake more cookies then, because I expect that every night. You know, with you living so close and all."

He glanced down at the cookies. "As for the gift size, you should know, based on your Santa-Steve present, that I appreciate ones from the heart."

"Oh! I haven't opened it yet!" I zipped over to the tree, where the gift was still stashed.

"You haven't?" His tone made me worry there was something time-sensitive inside.

"I wanted to wait until you were here with me, and then I was too mad to open it," I admitted.

We took a seat beside each other on the couch, and as I peeled off the wrapping paper, Steve's leg jiggled nervously. I paused and looked at him.

"It's not a ring, is it?" I teased.

He paled and shook his head.

His leg-jiggling continued.

Inside was a gift card to the college's bookstore, freshly ground coffee labeled for all-nighters, pens, a memory stick, a babysitting coupon from him, as well as an envelope with my name written in his tight scrawl. It held a coupon for a helicopter ride for when I needed perspective.

My eyes dampened at his thoughtfulness, his generosity, and the way I felt we were playing on the same field at last. Taking a deep breath, I wrapped him in my arms and kissed him slowly.

Steve, for all his flaws, was the right man for me, and I knew I would never want anyone else. I couldn't wait to explore all that made him the man I loved.

"I think I'm going to like the fact that you moved in next door." I waved the babysitting coupon and he laughed.

His expression became somber. "Are you going to tell Max we're dating?"

"Is that what we're doing?"

"Yes."

"Good, because I plan on introducing myself to everyone as your girlfriend. And, yes, I'll tell him."

Steve held me tighter so he could kiss me slowly. "If we were in a romantic comedy, I do believe it would be one of those stories where enemies become lovers."

I laughed again. There were a lot of things to look forward to when it came to being Steve Jorgensen's girlfriend.

* * *

Thank you for reading UNEXPECTEDLY IN LOVE. I hope you enjoyed Steve and Joy's love story. Want to know more about Joy's friend Cassandra, and how Cassandra's sister Alexa fell in love with her boss? Find out in her delightful Christmas short story SWEET HOLIDAY SURPRISE!

Rule Number One: Never date the boss.

Given Alexa's crash and burn history with office romances, it should be an easy rule to follow. Then again, her rules have never gone up against Cash Campbell. And especially not at a resort wedding in the romantic, oceanside town of Indigo Bay!

Find Alexa's story, SWEET HOLIDAY SURPRISE, as an ebook in your favorite online bookstore.

SIGN UP FOR Jean's newsletter to stay in the know about deals, new books and more! www.jeanoram.com/signup

ALSO BY JEAN ORAM

~ VEILS AND VOWS SERIES ~

Marriages of convenience in one nosy little town—you know things are going to get *good*!

- The Promise
- The Surprise Wedding
- A Pinch of Commitment
- The Wedding Plan
- Accidentally Married
- The Marriage Pledge
- Mail Order Soulmate

Psst! Did you know Jean's newsletter subscribers get *The Promise* for free? I know! How awesome is that? So quick! Get your name on her newsletter list and get the latest news as well as your book at www.jeanoram.com/freebook

ALSO BY JEAN ORAM

~ THE SUMMER SISTERS SERIES ~

Taming billionaires has never been so *sweet*.

* Available in paperback, audio & ebook *

One cottage. Four sisters. And four billionaires who will sweep them off their feet.

Falling for the Movie Star

Falling for the Boss

Falling for the Single Dad

Falling for the Bodyguard

Falling for the Firefighter

Check your favorite online bookstore for box sets, too!

Check out the entire series:

www.jeanoram.com/books/summer-sisters

ABOUT JEAN ORAM

Jean Oram is a *New York Times* and *USA Today* bestselling romance author who loves making opposites attract in tear-jerking, feel-good, sweet romances set in small towns. She grew up in a town of 100 (cats and dogs not included) and owns one pair of high heels which she has worn approximately three times in the past twenty years. Jean lives near a lake in Canada with her husband, two kids, cat, dog and those pesky deer who keep wandering into her yard to eat her rose bushes and apple trees.

Become an Official Fan: www.facebook.com/groups/jeanoramfans

Newsletter: www.jeanoram.com/signup

Twitter: www.twitter.com/jeanoram

Facebook: www.facebook.com/JeanOramAuthor

Instagram: www.instagram.com/Author_JeanOram

Website & blog: www.jeanoram.com

CPSIA information can be obtained
at www.ICGtesting.com
Printed in the USA
BVHW080801030121
596864BV00013B/621

9 781989 359068